D0756791

THE HEALER'S BLADE

WRAK-AYYA: THE AGE OF SHADOWS
BOOK FOUR

LEIGH ROBERTS

CONTENTS

Copyright © 2019 Leigh Roberts Author

All rights reserved. No part of this book may be reproduced or
transmitted in any form or by any means, electronic or mechanical,
including photocopying and recording, or by any information
storage and retrieval system, without permission in writing from the
Copyright owner.

Warning: the unauthorized reproduction or distribution of this
copyrighted work is illegal.

This is a work of fiction. Names, places, characters, creatures, and
incidents are either the product of the author's imagination or are
used fictitiously, and any resemblance to any actual persons,
creatures, living or dead, organizations, events, or locales is entirely
coincidental.

Editing by Joy Sephton http://www.justemagine.biz
Cover design by Cherie Fox http://www.cheriefox.com

Sexual activities or events in this book are intended for adults.

ISBN: 978-1-951528-03-4 (ebook)
ISBN: 978-1-951528-16-4 (paperback)

Dedication

*For everyone who still believes in the possibilities
answered by...*

What If?

CHAPTER 1

It was a daunting task. It had been a long time since the last full-scale pairing celebration, so record numbers of the People would be traveling to Kthama, the home of the People of the High Rocks, for this Ashwea Awhidi.

Living quarters, food stores, seating, watchers, guards, cleaning up; a multitude of logistics had to be planned and then executed.

In addition to providing enough housing for everyone, Acaraho, Kthama's High Protector, was concerned with the travel routes and ensuring that any Waschini, or White people, would not see those traveling above ground.

So far, the Waschini activity had not escalated as feared, and Acaraho knew Khon'Tor, Leader of the People of the High Rocks, was relieved he had not had to respond to increased Waschini presence by invoking Wrak-Ayya: the Age of Shadows. It was a good thing, as the constraints it would have placed on the People would make conducting an event of this magnitude far more complicated than it was already promising to be.

Still, not one to tempt fate, Acaraho would be stationing a full complement of watchers and guards along the routes from the outlying communities.

The People of the Great Pines and the High Red Rocks would be attending at the High Council's request. Because of the great distance, they generally did not participate in the pairing ceremonies of the communities situated, like Kthama, near the Mother Stream.

Everyone was happy at this exciting news, but it also meant the High Council was widening the pairing pool. Despite the efforts to ensure diverse pairings, at some point it was necessary to bring in new blood. For those communities of the People to travel this far across Etera only underscored that imperative.

Many of those coming would bring food supplies because everyone recognized the strain it created on a community to host such an event. However, the High Rocks food stores would still be hard hit. A bountiful harvest would replenish their depleted foodstuffs but would also require more work to bring in, process, and store.

The Healer and her Helper, Nadiwani, would be

busy all year, ensuring they had sufficient medical supplies on hand. The People were generally very healthy, but there was also the unexpected errant cut or wound—or worse.

Spirits were high despite all the impending work. Though the culmination would be the pairing announcements, there would also be socializing, storytelling, and reunions between the structured events.

Some pairings were more amiable than others, and not every paired couple shared living quarters. For some, it was an arrangement of procreation with little other involvement. These partners mostly lived in the gender-specific communal areas and came together only for physical enjoyment or release, or to produce offspring. Those who did develop close ties would request living quarters and share their lives on a long-term basis.

There was even a place for those who preferred to keep to themselves. Being a watcher was the perfect assignment for those loners who did not particularly enjoy community living—many of them staying out on their own for long stretches. These males were adept at hunting and locating food and water sources as well as finding cover from the elements if need be. In many cases, the males who chose to be watchers had a more highly developed sixth sense, making them even more sensitive than most to Etera's magnetic currents, by which they navigated and kept their bearings. They ventured into the community only to report to Acaraho or the First Guard, Awan, and in the case of those who were paired, briefly to visit their mates.

Akule was practically beside himself with anticipation. He was one of the adult unpaired bachelors and had struggled for years with the idea of taking a mate. It was the relationship between Acaraho and Adia, the Healer, that had changed his mind, though, other than the relationship between Khon'Tor and his long-dead mate, Hakani, none of the pairings in the community contained any animosity.

Matching the relationship expectations of those to be paired was of utmost importance to the High Council. For this reason, it was not always possible to find a match between the available candidates. However, this being a banner year for pairing, and considering the participation of the more-remote communities, Akule was hopeful that he would be paired this time around.

He was a watcher, but he longed to settle down and have the companionship he saw between Acaraho and Adia. Though they were not formally paired, everyone treated them as a couple and saw them as such.

Along with everyone else, Akule knew that

Healers were not permitted to pair or have offspring, but the scandal caused by Adia's adoption of the abandoned Waschini offspring, Oh'Dar, and then delivering her own offspring, Nootau, had long since died down. Oh'Dar had since left Kthama in search of his Waschini family, but Akule wondered if the existence of Nootau would become a popular topic because of its shock value to the members of the other communities.

Though it was not the case, no one doubted that Acaraho had fathered Nootau, including Nootau himself. The offspring, now almost fully grown, had the same build, the same strong, yet amiable personality. He was even picking up Acaraho's quick, but kindly wit, and the love between them was obvious. Acaraho had passed on his standards and expectations of how to treat others, the importance of doing one's best, pride in excellence, and kindness to those less fortunate.

Akule hoped to have a relationship like this with his own son one day.

Khon'Tor was pleased that so many from his community had asked to be paired, especially considering there would be matches made with others from so far away.

As Leader, he would be expected to make goodwill visits to neighboring communities. Travel along the Mother Stream was a safe and enjoyable route. Because it was straightforward, it would provide ample thinking time and a break from the demands of his usual responsibilities. Acaraho would accompany him to some of the communities to learn first-hand how many would be coming, among other logistical information.

◯

While his family back at Kthama was preparing for the upcoming celebration, Oh'Dar was preparing to travel to where he could receive advanced medical instruction before returning to apprentice with Dr. Miller.

With nothing to do but study and learn, Oh'Dar had made unprecedented progress. His first teacher, Miss Blain, had done an excellent job in grounding him in the fundamentals of reading and arithmetic. His current tutor, Mr. Carter, said Oh'Dar's mind was quick and sharp and that he'd be ready to leave by fall, able to become a doctor if he wished.

It had been some time since the attractive Miss Blain returned to her home. He never heard from her, though he continued to think about her and wondered if she ever thought about him. But another romance was blossoming under his eyes, one that made him very happy.

Oh'Dar was still nervous about leaving his

Waschini grandmother and traveling so far away. He'd already been through so many changes. He left Kthama to try and find his place in the world, and so far, it had been nothing but one different thing after another. It had started when the Webb Family welcomed him into their home, then he'd moved into his grandmother's home, Shadow Ridge, learned under two teachers, and now had the prospect of a whole new experience in yet another place.

Oh'Dar wanted his life to settle down. He missed the routine of the High Rocks, and he missed his mother and father, Nootau, and Kweeuu, his wolf cub. Oh, how he wished he had Kweeuu with him. The cub would be a massive, full-grown wolf by now. Oh'Dar wondered if he was still at Kthama or if his adult drives had called him off to other interests.

From what Oh'Dar had seen, some of the Waschini lived very differently than the People. Instead of making their supplies, his grandmother purchased most of hers locally. They did not spend time fashioning tools from the natural materials around them. They lived in smaller family units instead of a wider community like Kthama. They were more interested in their clothing and had quite a few different choices. Oh'Dar's collection of wrappings had also grown. His favorites were the black riding boots and black leather hat—he still did not like wearing the

Waschini boots or shoes, but women he met told him he looked handsome in them.

Oh'Dar had never considered himself handsome. Nootau was handsome, Acaraho was handsome, and Khon'Tor was handsome—if he understood the word to mean that females' eyes followed them wherever they went.

His viewpoint had expanded, however. He had found Miss Blain attractive. And he had come to recognize that his grandmother was considered attractive too, even though she was older, and that Mr. Jenkins seemed to think so as well.

Perhaps out of loyalty to her deceased husband— the man who had hired him—Mr. Jenkins had never acknowledged his affection for Mrs. Morgan. But Oh'Dar teased him about it and noticed the stable master had started making excuses to come up to the house to speak with his grandmother over one thing or another. She didn't seem to mind; in fact, she appeared to be wearing more feminine, softer colors, instead of the dark tones Oh'Dar had always known her to wear.

Oh'Dar was, however, fairly naive. He had known how to kiss Miss Blain because he had seen paired couples in the community do something similar, and something primal within him craved the feel of her in his arms and the feel of her lips on his. But as to what went on in private between a male and a female, he was somewhat unsure.

The People protected their offspring from adult

subjects. Only when they were of pairing age, and had asked to be paired, were the intimacies of what took place between a male and a female explained. Though they often witnessed certain public exchanges between paired couples, the offspring had no informed understanding other than what they observed among the forest creatures.

It was difficult for Oh'Dar, dealing with changes in his body and urges which he did not know how to deal with—urges which Miss Blain had brought painfully to the surface. The strict directive that the People's offspring be kept ignorant was designed to prevent sexual experimentation, lest unpaired seedings took place. It worked, but now Oh'Dar had questions, and here with the Waschini there was no Acaraho to reassure him and no preparatory Ashwea Tare for him to attend.

Oh'Dar often wondered about his brother, Nootau. Nootau would be ready to be paired by now if he wished. Once an offspring reached sexual maturity, it was best to be paired if a match could be found. Some chose not to be paired, but most did not wait long. Oh'Dar was confident that, based on the loving relationship they had both witnessed between their mother and father, Nootau would want to live with his mate.

Many nights as young brothers, Oh'Dar and Nootau had lain out under the stars that watched over Etera, wondering to each other why their mother and father did not live together. They understood that by law, they were not able to, but the community seemed to accept them as a pair, which confused the young males. Later, when they asked Acaraho about it, he explained that it was a matter of honor and respect for the rules, and that the community had already extended them a lot of leeway in their relationship as it was. But both Oh'Dar and Nootau were sure they would all be happier if they could have lived in the same quarters.

All these thoughts came to Oh'Dar as he lay in bed at night, missing his first home. He wished he could send a message that he was alright. He knew his mother and father would still be wondering what had happened to him.

Now that some time had passed, Oh'Dar found himself dealing with a new emotion that frightened him. Though he had done the man no harm, Louis had tried to kill him. And not only at the stables; it was Louis who had hired other men years before to kill them all, him *and* his parents. True, those parents were only pictures in the locket Adia had kept for him, and a sadness in his grandmother's smile, but they were still his parents. And he found he was angry at what his uncle had done.

It was not that he had never been angry before. He had certainly been angry at the secret bullying he received from Kahrock, a childhood peer, growing up. He had been angry that he was powerless to confront Kahrok directly and had to depend on Nootau's protection. But that was nothing like the visceral reaction he was now experiencing to what Louis had tried to do.

Oh'Dar had come to the Waschini to find answers but now only had more questions. If his Uncle had not had his birth parents killed, Oh'Dar would never have been rescued by his mother, Adia, who had always told him that she believed the Great Mother had given him to her for a reason. He would have had an entirely different life here among the Waschini, never knowing about the People. But then he would also never have been an Outsider at Kthama. Knowing what he knew now, would he change the past if he could?

All my life, I have strived to be the best at everything I could. Was that my way of trying to make a place for myself with the People? To prove my value and that I had a right to be there among them? To prove that I wasn't one of the White Wasters I heard whispered about? And yet here is anger within me at a level I have never experienced. Am I one of them, after all?

And what if Louis had succeeded in murdering me? None of them would ever know what had happened to me. Mama, Acaraho, Nadiwani, Nootau—they would all think I had just gone off and forgotten about them entirely. As if they meant nothing to me. That thought pierced Oh'Dar through the heart. He pinched his eyes shut tight and clenched his fists with resolve.

I must go back to Kthama. I must see them and tell them why I left. Even if Khon'Tor doesn't want me there, I must go home. Maybe my mother was right; maybe Khon'Tor was wrong, and I am not a threat to the People.

Oh'Dar knew it would devastate his grandmother if he left, even for a while. *I have to trust the Great Spirit that Grandmother will understand and that somehow, I will know when it is time. That some way will be opened for me to go.*

He lay awake night after night, wondering if he did belong anywhere and if he would ever find that place.

He lay awake night after night, wondering if he did belong anywhere and if he would ever find that place.

It was a warm summer morning when Oh'Dar first noticed something wrong. He was feeling off. He didn't want to eat, his whole body was hurting, and he was so tired. He told Mrs. Thomas that he wanted to stay in bed and asked her to tell his grandmother, Mr. Carter, and Mr. Jenkins, that he would not be joining them.

Mrs. Thomas went to find her employer. "Good morning, Mrs. Morgan; Grayson is not feeling well and is not up to his lessons today with Mr. Carter."

"Oh, dear, what's wrong?" asked Mrs. Morgan.

"I don't know. It could be some type of influenza. He has all the general symptoms. I think I remember Mr. Carter complaining a couple of weeks ago about not feeling well. Do you want me also to let Mr. Jenkins know?" asked Mrs. Thomas.

"No, thank you, I'll go and speak with him myself."

Mrs. Thomas could not help but smile.

Mr. Jenkins was coming out of the crew quarters and up the hill toward the barn when he spotted Mrs. Morgan. *Now, what brings her out this early?* he thought, though he was pleased to see her. She was carrying a small plate of something.

"Good morning, Jenkins. I thought you might like some warm biscuits. Mrs. Thomas just took them out of the oven." As she handed him the plate, Mr. Jenkins made sure his hand managed to brush hers.

Mrs. Morgan blushed, and a little smile crossed her lips. She was still a beautiful woman. Her auburn hair was thick and lush. She had a glowing complexion, and though she was heavier than in her youth, Mr. Jenkins found her curvy figure inviting.

"I must also tell you that Grayson isn't feeling well and won't be out to help you today. If it doesn't clear up in a day or so, I'll send for Dr. Miller," she explained.

"I'm sorry to hear that, Miss Vivian; thank you for telling me. You know, I think this is the first time the boy has ever been sick," he added.

Oh'Dar was no longer a boy, though for the most part, they still thought of him as such.

"I know. Grayson's very healthy. But about a week ago, Mr. Carter was complaining of not feeling well, so perhaps he brought something with him from town."

"Well, keep me posted and let me know if there is anything I can do," he said.

Mrs. Morgan started to walk away and then turned back, "Come to think of it, I do know of something you can do. Grayson is very fond of you, Jenkins. You know that; you've become a father figure to him. I think he's struggling with going away to school. I know you spend a lot of time with him, but perhaps it would be good for you to spend even more. Why don't you start coming up to the house in the mornings for breakfast? If you don't mind, of course," she added.

"I would be glad to. Thank you for your hospitality. Let me know when Master Grayson starts feeling better, and I'll make a point of it."

Mrs. Morgan's invitation was to put a little skip in Mr. Jenkins' step for several days to come.

❂

Oh'Dar languished. Mrs. Morgan sent someone to town, and before too long, the carriage returned with Dr. Miller.

After examining Oh'Dar, Dr. Miller came out to update Mrs. Morgan. "I've seen this before. It usually runs through the whole family when it hits. Most children get it early, and it's not serious. It can be harmful to adults, though. I'll check my charts when

I get back to the office, but from what I remember, everyone here went through it a long time ago. Even you, Mrs. Morgan."

Mrs. Morgan was relieved to hear it was unlikely anyone else would come down with it, but she was concerned for her grandson. "You said it can be serious for adults? Does this mean Grayson is in danger?" Alarm was creeping into her voice.

"It can be serious. So far, I don't see any signs of that. If it weren't for the swelling below Master Grayson's ears, it would easily be mistaken for a general ailment. But this can last up to three weeks. As long as there isn't any other swelling, he should be fine," explained Dr. Miller.

Mrs. Morgan needed a straight answer. "Dr. Miller, what is the worst thing that could happen to my grandson because of this?"

"The worst thing? That he might not be able to father children."

Dr. Miller then took gentle hold of Mrs. Morgan's arm to make sure she was listening. "But! As I said, he doesn't seem to have a severe case, and as long as there isn't inflammation anywhere else, he should recover just fine. And it doesn't always cause infertility. It's just a more serious disease in adults than in children." Dr. Miller went on to explain delicately what the signs would be should it turn serious.

Somewhat reassured, Mrs. Morgan had Dr. Miller taken back into town.

And Dr. Miller was right. The illness did not

seem to get much worse, nor did any complications seem to arise, and within three weeks, Oh'Dar was as good as new.

It was Oh'Dar's first bout with illness. The People were remarkably healthy, as were the Brothers. It was only in coming to live with the Waschini that he had seen people becoming ill—but having experienced it reinforced his desire to become a Healer like his mother, like Dr. Miller.

Planning and more planning continued for Oh'Dar's advanced instruction. Mrs. Morgan spent a lot of time writing to the hospital he would be going to, trying to ensure as easy a transition as possible for him. She knew it would be very different from his schooling. He would be with other students following the doctors around from case to case, listening, and asking questions.

"I found a boarding house not far from the hospital," she said to Mrs. Thomas as she sipped the tea her housekeeper had brought. "He will attend a series of specialized lectures. They hold them at the hospital so they can talk about the patients. He will still have to apprentice to Dr. Miller. But I don't think he will be gone as long as I had originally thought," she said, smiling.

After Oh'Dar had recovered enough to rejoin regular activities, he was pleased to see Mr. Jenkins at both the breakfast table and the evening dinner table. He wasn't sure how this had come about, but it gladdened him.

Oh'Dar was in his usual spot to one side of his grandmother, and Mr. Jenkins was in the other. In Oh'Dar's opinion, there was a natural fit to it.

"It's good to see you up and about, son." Mr. Jenkins often addressed him as son, which Oh'Dar had learned was a term of endearment.

"It's good to see you here, Mr. Jenkins!" exclaimed Oh'Dar with all sincerity. *With me gone, maybe they'll get even closer. The house will be almost empty then—*

Oh'Dar knew that Mr. Jenkins had worked for his grandmother for a long time. Oh'Dar's grandfather, the first Grayson Stone Morgan, had hired him. After Mr. Morgan passed, Mr. Jenkins had taken over most of the responsibility for running the ranch. Oh'Dar wondered if perhaps Mr. Jenkins had secretly harbored feelings for his grandmother for some time.

He watched the sweet exchange between them over dinner conversation and exchanged a little smile with whichever of the kitchen help came to clear the plates from the table.

Feigning fatigue, Oh'Dar usually excused himself early, leaving them to continue their conversation privately.

The obvious affection between them reminded him of Adia and Acaraho back home. He hoped that someday he would have a loving companion with whom to share his life. From everything he'd seen, being paired to someone you loved and who loved you in return was what brought happiness, not where you lived, or to a point, even how you lived.

Up in his room, he lay on his bed thinking of Miss Bain. Because she lived so far away, he doubted he would ever see her again.

CHAPTER 2

As the time drew closer, Khon'Tor prepared to visit the Leaders of the neighboring communities. Ordinarily, Acaraho should have accompanied him, but Khon'Tor did not want the High Protector's company and excused him. So, Acaraho put together the questions for which they needed answers, mostly concerning the number of people coming and what they would be bringing, if anything, to supplement what was available at Kthama.

Khon'Tor prepared his travel supplies. He ordinarily traveled light, but this time, in addition to food he packed gifts for the other Leaders. Khon'Tor was looking forward to his visits. Travel along the Mother Stream would be easy, and he would have a lot of time to think—and plan.

He told Acaraho that he was not sure just how long he would be gone. He would be traveling to both the People of the Far High Hills and the People of the Deep Valley as well as the small community where Kurak'Kahn' the High Council Overseer lived. In Khon'Tor's absence, Acaraho was in charge.

Khon'Tor set out early one day for the first community along the Mother Stream—the People of the Deep Valley, where Adia had originally come from. The People of the Deep Valley lived in the caves of Awenasa, which were very similar to Kthama, and which had probably made the transition a little easier for Adia. Their Leader was Lesharo'Mok, brother to Adia's father, Apenimon. Because Apenimon'Mok had died with no male offspring, his leadership had passed to a male blood relative.

As he walked, Khon'Tor let his mind wander, and he reflected on the past few years. After the death of Hakani, everything had shifted for him. Acaraho and Adia were in the seat of power, and Khon'Tor's position existed only at their will and mercy. Should Adia at any time reveal that he was Nootau's father and how that had come about, Khon'Tor would lose his position as Leader—and more.

None of that helped to mitigate his anger at Adia. Despite everything, he still blamed her for his problems. He might not be able to take revenge on her directly, but there could be a next-best thing.

The Deep Valley was several days' travel along the Mother Stream, and he enjoyed the solitude. Whoever of the Ancients had lived in these caves long ago, and modified the passageway along the Mother Stream, had taken long travel along its route into consideration. There were many places to stop, rest, and sleep along the way. Time became lost underground, but markings on the walls gave estimates as to how much distance remained.

Along the route, there were entrances to the Mother Stream. Acaraho had stationed guards at those near the High Rocks when the problems with the Waschini arose. Once past those, there were no more entrances until close to the next stop—which was the small community among which Kurak'Kahn, the High Council Overseer, lived. Khon'Tor would stop there on his return trip after he had met with Lesharo'Mok of the Deep Valley, and Harak'Sar, Leader of the Far High Hills.

Lesharo'Mok's leadership style was similar to that of his deceased brother, Apenimon. Both led their community with a gentle approach, tempering the First and Second Laws with the Third of the First Laws that required forbearance for each other's failings. Harak'Sar of the Far High Hills, on the other hand, was similar to Khon'Tor in temperament and ruled with a far stronger hand.

Khon'Tor hoped he had laid his additional plans well because he would not have another opportunity for a very long time. He had left things open, knowing that not everything would necessarily come off smoothly, and he that might have to extend his stay for longer than he intended. He had to be very careful. He had spent many nights over the past several months thinking it through and felt he had covered every contingency, but there was always the chance of something going wrong. If it looked at any point as if he would not succeed, Khon'Tor was ready to abandon his plans. There was too much to lose if he failed, no matter how attractive the reward.

He passed the exit that led to the Overseer's home. Khon'Tor had no plans for this small community, other than to stop on the return trip and tell Kurak'Kahn what he had learned from the other Leaders. He had traveled for several days and there were more to go.

Khon'Tor carefully noted the stopping off points along the way—the particularly comfortable sleeping spots, the alcoves designed for personal care, and the shallow bathing pools. Drinking water was no problem, and he had more than enough food for the journey.

As he approached the underground branch that led to the community of the Deep Valley, Khon'Tor took particular note of the nooks and crannies. Because it was farther out, their territory had not been encroached on by the Waschini, so there were no guards posted at the exit points that led above ground. Like the entrance to Kthama and Awenasa, the openings were very well hidden. Without knowing they were there, or seeing someone exit, it would be impossible to discover them. The Ancients had done well by the People in all known regards.

As he got closer to Awenasa, Khon'Tor passed several females gathering water. The Mother Stream provided an inexhaustible supply of fresh water, as well as oxygen for the underground living system. Just as with Kthama, it wound through the lower levels of Awenasa.

The females paused as Khon'Tor approached. They had heard he was coming, and they recognized him by his silver crown and imposing physical attributes. He nodded a greeting to them and continued on, aware of how their eyes passed over him appreciatively. After he had passed, he heard them whispering about him in eager tones.

As he entered the lower levels of Awenasa, the markings indicated the route to the main level. Again, he passed several of the community who were excited at his presence.

Finally, he came across one of the guards who escorted him to the main area to find Lesharo'Mok. The Leader of the People of the Deep Valley was sitting among some of his males in a meeting when the guard brought Khon'Tor over.

Lesharo'Mok rose with a greeting, glad his counterpart had arrived in the morning and not in the small hours of the night. "Welcome, Khon'Tor of the High Rocks. We are glad to provide hospitality to you. Your temporary quarters have been ready for some time. Would you like to make yourself at home before we meet?"

"Thank you, Lesharo'Mok; I would. It has been many days' travel. I could appreciate a decent meal. Nuts and dried berries only do for so long in satisfying a male's appetite," Khon'Tor explained. *Speaking of appetites*—Khon'Tor let his eyes wander over the female standing next to Lesharo'Mok.

"Tar'sa here will show you to your quarters, and I will have someone bring you a hearty midday meal. If you would like, you can join me later for the evening meal in the community eating hall. Tar'sa will point it out on the way to your quarters, and I will send someone to check on you when it is time. I hope you will find everything satisfactory."

When Lesharo'Mok had finished speaking, Tar'sa led Khon'Tor to his room.

Lesharo'Mok had made sure that the room was very comfortable, and Khon'Tor immediately spotted the generously prepared sleeping mat. He was looking forward to stretching out in the luxurious spot and getting some real rest before the meeting.

Like everything at Kthama, the rooms, corridors, and even doorways of Awenasa were oversized. Khon'Tor often wondered about the size of the Ancients who had made their underground dwellings to such large proportions. He knew the Sarnonn were larger than the People, though it had been generations since any of the People had encountered one, but it still seemed out of proportion.

Khon'Tor took out the gift for Lesharo'Mok. He was glad to lighten his carrying satchel, but he made sure the other items he had brought were secure before putting it all aside.

Before too long, the young female returned, bringing food to Khon'Tor's new quarters. He eyed her as she came in and set it down near where he was resting. He wondered if all the females of the Deep Valley were so attractive. He tried to conceal his admiration of her attributes, but he could tell from her reaction that he had not been as discreet as he had thought. He started to become aroused, but told himself, *be patient. Soon—hopefully, soon.*

After the female left, Khon'Tor devoured the meal and then rested. Quite a while later, Tar'sa returned to let him know that it was almost time for the evening meal, to which Adoeete Lesharo'Mok was expecting him.

As she was leaving, Khon'Tor stopped her. "What is your name?" he asked, though he knew it. He could see by her reaction that his deep voice was as pleasing to her as the rest of him.

"Tar'sa," she replied.

"Thank you, Tar'sa. I hope I will see more of you during my visit here," he replied.

Tar'sa blushed, flattered. Obviously, he did not know that she was paired. She merely nodded and said she would wait outside for him to get ready and would escort him to the general eating area.

○

Being noticed by a Leader such as Khon'Tor of the People of the High Rocks was about the most flattering thing that had happened to Tar'sa in a long time. She had heard of his striking looks, but in person he exceeded her imagination.

When she came into his quarters, she had intended to leave the food on the worktable, but he was stretched out on the bed, resting, and she thought it might be rude to put it so far out of reach. She walked to where he was reclining and set the tray down on the floor next to him.

Tar'sa was paired, but she could still not help but notice him and how his eyes lingered over her while she set the tray down. Had she not been paired she would have flirted with him in hopes of encouraging his interest. She had heard he was finally seeking a new mate all these years after the death of his first.

○

Khon'Tor and Lesharo'Mok enjoyed their meal together and talked about the upcoming pairing ceremony. Khon'Tor got the answers Acaraho wanted regarding how many would be traveling to Kthama, if they would be bringing supplies, and what else they might need to be provided with. He presented Lesharo'Mok with the gift he had brought him—a gourd filled with the sweetest clover honey available from their area. It was a great delicacy, and Lesharo'Mok thanked him.

Lesharo'Mok had been at the High Council meeting when Adia confessed her sin of breaking the Second Law, that Healers may never produce offspring. He had heard Khon'Tor's inspiring defense of her. He had also seen the tension between Khon'Tor and his mate, Hakani. He suspected that Hakani's death had not brought any heartbreak to Khon'Tor, though he did wonder why he had waited so long before taking another mate.

Their meeting done, Khon'Tor did have one question for his counterpart. "Lesharo'Mok, may I inquire about the female Tar'sa? The one who has been assigned to make my stay comfortable. Is she paired?"

"She is a beautiful female, is she not? So many of our females are; I am not sure why we are so blessed. No, I am sorry, Tar'sa is not available. She is indeed paired and has been for a few years now."

"Well, her mate is fortunate, to be sure. I will be leaving in the morning to continue on my journey, and I would like to thank her for her kindness. Do you know where I might find her in the morning before I set out?"

"I will be sure to tell her, Khon'Tor. But most

mornings she gathers water at the Mother Stream if you wish to tell her yourself," he explained.

Khon'Tor spent a few more minutes with Lesharo'Mok, asking general polite questions about Tar'sa's family.

After a while, he thanked the Leader of the Deep Valley, and added, "I look forward to seeing you at Kthama for the pairing celebration. Do you mind if I stop again on my way back? I want to meet those of your females who are available for pairing."

"Of course. I will let the maidens know that you would like to meet them," he replied. Khon'Tor was legendary. He could only imagine their excitement when he told them that they were going to meet the great Khon'Tor—and at his request!

Khon'Tor retired to his room. Thinking about Tar'sa, he had trouble sleeping that night. A terrible risk—it would be a terrible risk. But Khon'Tor had waited too long. He would not be able to wait for his new mate to produce offspring before he could take a female in the way that he wanted.

Khon'Tor set out early the next morning, down through the levels of Awenasa to the Mother Stream. He set out back in the direction of the High Rocks, instead of continuing toward his next stop, the Far High Hills. Finding a niche that provided him with a long view of the winding stream, he waited.

One, two, three days Khon'Tor hid in the tunnels of the Mother Stream—each morning watching Tar'sa. Finally, by the fourth day, he knew her pattern and those of the females who came later. Enough time had passed—no one would suspect he was still in the area.

Before too long, Tar'sa came to collect her day's water supply. He watched her, his eyes covering her hungrily.

Tar'sa knelt to dip her container in the moving stream. As she waited for it to fill, she thought about Khon'Tor, the Leader of the People of the High Rocks —his muscular chest, his strong thighs, his imposing presence. She knew she should not be nursing such thoughts, but she told herself it was harmless enough.

As she rose to leave, her water container filled, she turned to find Khon'Tor standing directly in front of her.

"Oh! Khon'Tor! Adoeete, what are you doing here still? I—we thought you left days ago?" she stammered. He was standing so close that she could feel the heat radiating off his huge frame.

Khon'Tor took the water container from her and set it down. He then very calmly took her hands and brought them together into one of his. "Oh, I know. But you see, I could not stop thinking about you,

Tar'sa. You are very beautiful, and I know you enjoyed it when I was looking at you." He continued to talk as he led her down the tunnel toward the niche in which he had been hiding.

"I do not understand. What—" she gasped, stumbling along with him, caught in his grasp.

"Sssh—you will understand in a moment. Just come with me," Khon'Tor answered.

"Adik'Tar 'Tor. Please, stop— Where are we going?" Her eyes darted around the surroundings. He was taking her somewhere *private*.

"We're just going to spend a little time together. Do not worry. I will try to make it enjoyable for you. I know it will be for me."

Her eyes widened as what she feared he had in mind was looking probable now. "Stop, please. I will scream!"

Khon'Tor paused and turned to face her. "If you scream, you will only make it worse for yourself. There is no one else coming down here. I have watched you for days. Just relax. It will be over in a few moments, and then you can return on your way," he said. "There is no need for this to get ugly," he added calmly.

She could feel his eyes watching her every move. *He must know he is hurting my wrists, and yet he does not care.* Tar'sa closed her eyes and willed herself to wake up. *Surely this is a nightmare. No male in his right mind would do what I think Khon'Tor is doing, and especially not someone in his position.*

He brought her into the little niche and pressed her up against the wall, and still with one hand, stretched both her arms over her head.

Helpless, Tar'sa felt Khon'Tor's free hand wander across and down her body, exploring all her soft areas. He took his time; he seemed to enjoy it when she tensed up in fear of where his hand would move next.

Tar'sa's mind was racing, wondering what the chances were that anyone would believe her. *It would be my word against the Leader of the High Rocks. If he is so bold as to do this, then who knows what else he might be capable of.*

She stopped hoping that someone would discover them, because she feared what he might do to them to cover up his crime.

"Does that not feel good, Tar'sa?" he taunted her, touching her gently. "Oh, you knew I was watching you. You knew, and you put on quite an enticing show. I am glad it worked out for us."

As he continued his exploration of her curves and private places, his touch became less gentle. "You must be tired of standing. Here, go ahead and kneel down."

Tar'sa knew there was no escaping. He was far too strong to fight off. Having weighed her choices, she realized there was nothing to do but endure whatever he was going to do to her.

As Tar'sa knelt, Khon'Tor lowered himself too, her hands still caught in his grasp.

"Now, I am going to let go. Please do not do anything foolish," he admonished.

She nodded that she understood. Her wrists were aching from his grip.

"Look at me," Khon'Tor ordered her.

When she complied, he said, "There, is this so terrible? Most females find me attractive, I am told. Is it so bad, the idea of being with me?" he asked, drawing a line with one finger all the way down the front of her.

There was no possible right answer. If Tar'sa said yes, she would anger him. If she said no, she would be giving her consent.

Khon'Tor lay down and patted the ground, signaling her to join him. Once she had also lain down, he rolled over and straddled her, one knee on each side of her legs.

"You did not answer me, Tar'sa. Is the idea of this —of me—really so repugnant?"

Either way, it was a win-win for Khon'Tor. *If I say yes, it will just make him angry. If I say no, then he can say I gave my consent.* She was silent.

Khon'Tor placed both hands on her hips and dragged her roughly to him. She tried to hide her fear because it seemed only to excite him further. *What is wrong with him?*

"No answer? Alright. We will play it that way then, and I will take that as a *yes*," he said, flashing an angry scowl. "Do you know how many females would trade places with you right now, given the chance? What is it with you, Tar'sa? Are you too good for me? Am I not *male* enough for you?" he said with a snarl.

"No! No! I mean, yes. *Yes!*" she cried out in fear at his angry display.

"I am glad to hear it. And I will take that as consent." Though it was a trick, technically, she had just consented.

Khon'Tor slipped one knee and then the other between her legs, grabbed her hips again and pulled her roughly the rest of the way against him. She turned her head and closed her eyes as he pressed his hard desire against her.

"No, no. Open your eyes and look at me, Tar'sa," he demanded.

She reluctantly opened her eyes as she was told and turned her head to make eye contact.

"Do not dare look away." Khon'Tor kept her locked in his gaze. It was clear he wanted to see her every reaction to what he was doing.

But as he made one swift forward motion and buried himself in her, she could not help it; she had to close her eyes in pain. He then took his enjoyment of her, rocking her hard in search of release from his years of deprivation. She was grateful it did not take him long to finish. But instead of pulling away from her, he kept his position.

She felt so small compared to him. He had her pinned captive with no way to wiggle out from under him.

He leaned over and whispered in her ear, "I am sorry it was so brief; I wanted to enjoy you a lot longer. It could not have been that good for you, I am sure. I promise it will be better next time."

Next time? Oh, no, not again! Despite knowing she had no chance against Khon'Tor, she still started to struggle. She pounded his chest with her fists. She tried to claw his face, but he easily blocked her attack. When he had so effortlessly subdued her, she started to cry. Too late, she realized that fighting him only inflamed him further.

"Oh, Tar'sa. Am I to take it there is not going to be a next time? I hope you will change your mind. But in case not, well, then we had better make the most of what we have now. And since you find it difficult to look at me, I will make it easy for you," and he flipped her over and pulled her up to her knees.

With one arm encircling her waist, he took her from behind, slamming himself into her, enjoying every little sound that escaped her lips. This time, he lasted longer, until he could not hold out anymore and again emptied himself into her.

When he was done, they both dropped to the grass. After a moment, he easily rolled Tar'sa over again so she could see him as he spoke to her. "I have to be going now. I am glad we had some time together. I hope you will change your mind about seeing me again. I will be back in a few days. Now, if you are smart—and I believe you are—though it will be uncomfortable, I strongly suggest that you mate with Knoton tonight."

"You know my mate's name?" she exclaimed.

"Oh, yes. And those of your mother and father and sister. So, if you care about them, you probably do not want to say anything about our little time together here this morning."

He was clearly threatening her, and she had no doubt he was serious. "Why would I mate—"

"Mate with Knoton tonight? Oh, come on, Tar'sa, think. Should you end up seeded, it would be best if there were a chance that it was his," he explained.

Tar'sa had been so scared that she had not thought past the moment. *What if I am seeded? It would be his word against mine. He is right. The best thing I can do now is to make sure that if I do, people assume it is Knoton's.*

Tar'sa realized then that this was not some random attack. Khon'Tor had planned and thought it out for a while. "May I go now?" she asked, wiping her tear-streaked face with the back of her hand.

"Of course. But remember—my reach is farther than you think. Do not do anything foolish. You have not lost anything except a little time. You were not a maiden. I hope you found some enjoyment in it. As long as you move on and let it go, I will not bother you again. Or your family," he said calmly.

"Now, pull yourself together and take it as a compliment," he added.

Tar'sa nodded; she would agree to anything to get

away from him. She knew there was nothing she could do about the attack. She had no proof, and she believed that his threats were real. She fled the little niche and then stopped and cleaned herself up before gathering her water container and being on her way. As she looked back, she knew he was watching her from the shadows.

Khon'Tor gathered up his things and continued on his path. Once he was farther down the tunnel, he stopped to rest and took some more pleasure revisiting his experience with Tar'sa. He relished the freedom from the tension he had been holding for so long; it was exquisite. He had forgotten how pleasurable it was. He was confident she would be silent, and he had been careful not to leave any marks when overpowering her. The fear in her eyes had been delicious—it was all about the conquest and the domination.

A few more days' travel and Khon'Tor reached the People of the Far High Hills. As before, he scouted the resting areas and alcoves as he drew nearer to the area.

Not all the People lived in expansive underground caves. Some lived in smaller, more nomadic groups. They followed the food supply and had no real structure as such. For established communities like the Deep Valley and the High Rocks, it was necessary to have a center for their activities and lifestyle.

The People of the Far High Hills did not live in an expansive underground system, but they did have a surface cave of considerable proportions. Separate smaller caves in the area were used for gender-specific living. They mostly foraged and hunted in small groups. The cohesive community structure that Khon'Tor's People enjoyed was the exception, not the norm.

Their primary cave extended into the mountain-side to quite an extent and provided shelter and the opportunity for the People of the Far High Hills to enjoy group activities and events.

Khon'Tor's arrival was just such an event. When he exited the underground system of the Mother Stream, he easily followed the markers to the main entrance. It was a considerable climb. He had only been here a few times, but the tree breaks kept him on the ancient trail. Several guards greeted him and took him in to meet Harak'Sar, their Leader.

Harak'Sar was much like Khon'Tor; strong-willed, driven. They had a natural understanding of each other. As with Lesharo'Mok, Harak'Sar had arranged pleasant sleeping quarters for Khon'Tor and bid him relax before the evening meal. Since he was not going to travel this way for some time,

Khon'Tor asked Harak'Sar if before he left, he could meet the maidens who were available for pairing at the upcoming ceremony.

With a twinkle in his eye, Harak'Sar said he would gladly make arrangements for them to meet Khon'Tor after the evening meal that night.

Khon'Tor was ready for a rest, though there was no exciting female taking care of his needs this time, only a young guard who brought him some niceties.

The cave of the People of the Far High Hills was far more open to the outdoors than Kthama. The entrance was mammoth, which let lots of light into the space, but also let a lot of the natural elements in. For that reason, most of the People stayed toward the far end, and down the corridors and in other small chambers. Visiting here made Khon'Tor realize just how fortunate his people were in having such an extensive underground living system.

As populations outgrew the available space, the overflow was forced to venture out and form new communities or to live in proximity to the primary population, but under less favorable conditions. The People of the High Hills were reaching their limit. They had a large number of maidens available to be paired—one way to restrict population growth because the females would go to live with the communities of their mates, and their offspring would, of course, become part of the new community.

An unpopular method of capitalizing on pairing

ceremonies was to place mating moratoriums across all communities so offspring would only be produced in cycles. A group of offspring of the same age was easier to pair than a group of different ages, because they were ready to be matched and relocated at the same time.

After their evening meal and business chat were over, twelve maidens were brought to where Harak'Sar and Khon'Tor were sitting and were introduced one by one.

Urilla Wuti, their escort and the community Healer, stood by the females and watched as Khon'Tor looked over each one. He was doing a terrible job of hiding his lust. The young females had lowered their eyes, only peeking at him occasionally. *They are flattered to be meeting the great Khon'Tor.*

Urilla Wuti did not need to use her seventh sense to pick up that his interest in the maidens was at the forefront of his visit. *He doesn't seem to recognize me, even though I stayed with Adia for months before her delivery. He has no idea that I know he is the father of Adia's offspring, or that I know he took her Without Her Consent.*

She saw his eyes lingering over each of them. *Is this just the normal interest of a virile male, or was his violation of Adia more than an isolated act of rage?* She knew though, that Adia would be watching over any female whom he chose to be his mate.

Khon'Tor asked the group of maidens to sit down. He enjoyed talking with them, analyzing their answers to his questions, trying to ascertain which was the most mild-mannered. Though he would not be able to pre-select from any of those coming from the farther regions, at least he would know who was available from the local communities.

By the end of the evening, Khon'Tor had selected three maidens with gentle personalities, any of whom he would pick. Though many of the People of Harak'Sar's community were lighter in coloring, one stood out. A young female with unusually lighter tones and honey-colored hair. Like the others, she wore light cover-ups, but in her case, they were a necessity because she was so fair. He felt drawn to her, but he could also make a selection from those of the Deep Valley, whom he would meet on his return trip.

Having seen a pool of candidates, he would avoid the mistake he had made with Adia by having only one maiden in his mind. Since the Leader had to wait for the pairing and other announcements to be done before he could make his selection, he did not want to be caught out again.

He sometimes thought that the Leader's pick should take precedence but understood that the High Council made each pairing only after great thought and deliberation. They strove to match the males and females by temperament and choice of living styles, with the first focus on their bloodlines for the health of the People. For a Leader to pluck a female from their selections could leave another male without a well-matched mate. And since being selected by a Leader was such a high honor, there was little risk of rejection by those remaining.

The proximity of these young maidens was stirring his appetites. He imagined restraining and exploring each one of them, feeling them squirm as they tried to get away from his probing attentions. He pictured the delicate honey-colored maiden pinned under him, his to do with as he pleased. His heart rate picked up; his body was reacting to his thoughts. As much as he did not want to squash the delicious tension rising within him, he had to calm himself.

The young females were mesmerized by Khon'Tor. He was frighteningly huge to them, far larger than any of the males in their community. Frightening, but also exciting in a manner they did not understand. As she was speaking to him, each maiden blushed at his admiration as he ran his eyes over her.

Harak'Sar noticed Khon'Tor's intense reaction to the females. *This male needs to take a mate, and soon*, he noted to himself.

Khon'Tor concluded his visit and prepared for his long trek back to Kthama. He had not rested well because his visit with the young females had stirred him up and kept him from sleep. He did not want to repeat his clandestine performance here at the Deep Valley. Well, he did, but he must not risk it. He could see no opportunity here to satisfy his need.

He still had in his satchel the items he had brought to this end. That he might not get to use them was disappointing, to say the least.

Khon'Tor found Harak'Sar and took his leave, remembering the gift of the clover honey before he went.

It was a brisk morning as he set out. The cooler weather made travel much easier than suffering the humid air of summer that made it hard to breathe.

A little way down the path toward the entrance to the Mother Stream, Khon'Tor realized that someone was following him. Along his left ran a large rock wall, to his right, thick underbrush. He knew that whoever it was must be behind him as there was no parallel path. When he stopped, they stopped.

He came across an indent in the rock wall and stepped into the shadows. He knew that whoever was behind him would realize that he had stopped, but counted on their curiosity causing them to continue.

Sure enough, whoever it was could not take the waiting and continued toward his hiding place. As they walked past, he reached out and quickly and surely dragged the figure into the recessed area.

He was surprised at the small stature of the male he had just overpowered. *Some young buck testing his mettle against the great Khon'Tor, no doubt*, he thought. He pushed the stalker up against the wall, trapping him, while at the same time covering his mouth with a huge hand.

In his anger, Khon'Tor pushed his captive's head back and pressed his canines against the exposed throat in a clear message. Then, releasing the pressure, he growled, "*Who are you, and why are you following me?*"

Waiting for the answer he removed his hand so the young male could speak, and looked down into widened eyes.

"I am sorry, Adik'Tar, I am sorry. I only wanted to talk to you some more," came the answer in the terrified voice of a young female.

He recognized her as one of the maidens he had met the night before. Still pressed against her, his body now responded to the realization that this was a female he had trapped against the rock wall and not some young male as he had first thought.

Khon'Tor quickly ran their location through his thoughts. How far away from the entrance had they walked? Did he remember seeing anyone else on this path when he arrived? Watchers? Other travelers?

"Is that why you followed me?" He asked a question with an obvious answer only to keep her talking while he thought.

"Yes, Adik'Tar. I am sorry. But I know you are

choosing a mate this Ashwea Awhidi, and I did not want you to forget me!" she volunteered.

Ordinarily, Khon'Tor was not interested in females who were interested in him; however, this was a different circumstance. This female had not followed him wanting to mate, but rather hoping to leave a lasting impression on him. He decided that her initiative should be commended—and *rewarded*.

His disappointment of a few hours ago quickly turned to delight as it appeared his lack of a plan had just been solved for him.

"I see. What is your name?" he asked, still pressed against her.

"Kayah." She was not uncomfortable, but his body pressing against her was suddenly feeling very intimate. What had first been a defensive reaction on his part was now changing into something totally different.

"Please, let me go. I am sorry I bothered you. I should not have followed you," she stammered.

"On the contrary, Kayah. There is nothing to be sorry about. Quite the opposite. I think that instead of being something to apologize for, I should reward your efforts," he said. "I remember our conversation last night. You seem like a bright young female, full of promise."

As he was talking, Khon'Tor started running one hand over her, beginning at her shoulder, then moving slowly across and down the front of her. He stopped to cup one of her mounds in his hand, making little circles around its tip with his thumb.

She tried to pull away. "Please, stop that. Please— I did not mean to— I mean—"

"Sssh. Just relax, Kayah. We are here now. It is just you and me. And I am glad you came; you are very beautiful."

His face was inches from hers. He was speaking so calmly, as if nothing out of the ordinary was happening.

He continued his hand's journey lower, finally coming to rest between her thighs. Kayah squirmed, trying to move away from his hand, but he had her pinned against the wall. She pushed against his chest, trying to free herself—her resistance only inflaming Khon'Tor's lust.

Unmoved by her efforts, he cupped her and then started to probe—giving her a preview of what was to come.

"Oh, no, nooooo." Kayah squirmed harder.

She was soft, warm, and enveloping—that is until he hit an obstruction. *Oh. That is right. She is a maiden*, he realized. No problem, this would just require a little more force—which was his specialty, after all.

"No, please. You cannot. You cannot!" She turned her head from side to side in alarm.

"Oh, Kayah. You are very wrong. I certainly can, and I certainly am going to. It was you who followed me. I did not approach you. I did not do anything but admire you from across a table and spend a pleasant evening talking with you and the other young females. It is you who sought *me* out. It is you who asked for this. I am just giving you what you came for, after all," he teased her.

"No, no. This is not what I wanted. I only wanted to talk to you some more. Please, do not do this."

Ignoring her, he continued calmly. "Seeing that you are a maiden, it is going to take a little more effort on my part to mate you. Do you understand?" he explained.

She did not acknowledge what he was saying, so he continued. "You are very beautiful, and I am going to enjoy this so much. Do not worry; I will go slowly. Since this is your first time, I want it to be memorable for you."

He spoke calmly. He had learned that the two ways in which to instill fear were to be very matter of fact or to outright terrify them. He preferred this first route, though growling and snarling produced a quicker result. "If you cry out, you will force me to hurt you. And make no mistake, I will if I must. Do you understand?"

She nodded.

He withdrew his hand and lifted Kayah, throwing her over his shoulder. While he carried her deeper into the recess, he enjoyed running his free hand over the curves of her exposed backside. Still not having surrendered, she beat her fists against his back as he carried her. Khon'Tor just smiled all the more.

He laid her down on a level spot and took his place next to her. He smoothed her hair back. She was so frightened that he knew little would calm her. While he continued to stroke her hair with one hand, he returned to exploring her with his other. "Well, I think you are almost ready for me, Kayah," he taunted her.

As he had with Tar'sa, he moved on top of her, placing first one knee and then the other between her legs to part them—creating the access to her that he needed.

He pressed against her, letting her feel his desire for her. She said no more words, but a moan of distress escaped her lips. He pressed himself into her, just the slightest amount until he met the resistance his fingers had found earlier. Oh, how he wished he could stop time. The anticipation of his next move was exquisite.

He could see she had turned her head away, eyes squeezed shut. "Look at me," he commanded. Kayah shook her head no and squeezed her eyes tighter.

"This *is* going to happen. There is nothing you can do about it. I suggest you look at me and do as I say. You cannot stop this. Your compliance now only determines how painful I make it for you," explained Khon'Tor.

She finally opened her eyes and looked at him. The reality of the situation hit her—she was about to be mated Without Her Consent by the most powerful of all the People's Leaders. No one would believe her. Her fear now bowed to her need for survival, and she complied with what he wanted.

Khon'Tor pressed himself a little farther into her. He saw her wince with pain. "Yes, yes, I know. It is going to be a little uncomfortable for you. Just take a deep breath and let it out slowly," he told her.

As she did, at the moment of her exhale, he thrust himself forward until he was fully seated within her. Kayah's entire body tensed against him. Her fingernails clawed into his back. She pushed against him with her legs. He held his position, deep within her.

As he had promised, he took his time with her. Moving slowly in and slowly out, the experience with Tar'sa not too many days before helped his self-restraint. But he knew he would still not be able to hold out for long, nor was it wise to draw it out as much as he wished to.

He noticed that she had closed her eyes again. No matter, he leaned over and placed the flat of his tongue against her neck and drew one long wet stroke up, ending at her ear, into which he whispered, "I am going to empty myself into you now, Kayah. Are you ready?" it was a rhetorical question because the point of no return was upon him, and in the next second, Khon'Tor delivered one last long, deep thrust. Sweet pulses of release blinded his consciousness to everything else.

He wanted to take a few moments to recover and take her again, but this was not as protected an area as it had been with Tar'sa. Reluctantly he decided that there would only be time for this one dance with Kayah.

Khon'Tor relaxed next to her for a short while, savoring the discharge of his long-suffered tension.

She lay unmoving, her arms crossed over and covering her eyes as tears rolled down the sides of her face.

He propped himself up on one arm and laid his hand on her belly. She rolled over to face away from him.

"Do not be like that, Kayah. Remember that you came to me. I was very gentle with you compared to how I could have been. And I saved your mate the trouble of dispensing with your maidenhead. It will go much easier for both you and him now. And if you are tempted to tell anyone about this—don't. They would not believe you, and there would be serious consequences." There was cold, authoritative steel in his voice now.

Then Khon'Tor switched tactics. He played with a curl of her hair. "Well, I need to be on my way. I trust you can find your path back safely? I look forward to seeing you in a few months at the celebration. And do not worry, if you do end up with offspring, you will not be far enough along to show. Just be sure you mate frequently when you are paired, from the first night. You can claim the offspring is premature if it comes to that."

He rose, then helped her to her feet and steadied her with one hand. He brushed her down and then gently wiped the tears from her face. Khon'Tor knew that because she was a female, his attentiveness would confuse her and mitigate her anger with him. When faced with conflicting treatment, most females let their reason be clouded by any kindness they were shown.

Khon'Tor led her back to the main path and watched her walk away. He was confident she would say nothing. She was a truly beautiful female, and he had thoroughly enjoyed her. It was a shame that she was now out of the running as his mate, because she had been one of the three he favored.

Any female *should* be thrilled to be chosen by Khon'Tor unless she knew what Tar'sa and Kayah now knew. The crowd would be expecting a surprised and excited response from the maiden he selected. He could not risk any other kind of public reaction at the time of his choosing.

As promised, Khon'Tor stopped back at the Deep Valley on his return trip. He wanted to meet the maidens who would be available. Since they had not known when he would return, Lesharo'Mok had kept his guest quarters available.

Khon'Tor was surprised to see it was again Tar'sa who was tending him. Obviously, she had kept her mouth shut as he had ordered.

After the evening meal with Lesharo'Mok, as at the Far High Hills the available maidens came to meet Khon'Tor. He had to admit that the Deep Valley had the most beautiful females, and he remembered that Adia had also come from this community.

They all seemed to have amiable personalities. Khon'Tor preferred a smaller mate, one more easily frightened. His thoughts kept returning to the honey-colored female who had seemed particularly sweet, in addition to being very beautiful. He found himself wondering what it would be like to tear off those wraps she wore.

Khon'Tor thanked them for their time and wished them all well in their upcoming pairing. He then retired to his quarters in preparation for leaving in the morning.

Before he slept, he spent some time in reflection. He had hesitated to take a mate because of Hakani's warning that no female would keep quiet about his need to subjugate her. Now he wondered if it were possible to combine fear and pleasure. He also realized that he and Hakani had hated each other, so hurting her added greatly to his pleasure. But with these females, for whom he felt no animosity, frightening them alone had been enough. If he started slowly and pleasured his new mate, and found the right combination of pleasing her and yet taking control, perhaps in time, he could train his new mate to enjoy being dominated—at least enough to keep it secret.

The tiny honey-colored female from the Far High Hills stayed in his thoughts.

CHAPTER 3

Khon'Tor headed back toward Kthama,
stopping first at the small community
where Kurak'Kahn, the High Council
Overseer, lived. Kurak'Kahn was pleased to receive
him and find out what Harak'Sar and Lesharo'Mok
had shared about the number of attendees they
would be sending.

"I have just come from the Deep Valley and the
Far High Hills. There is a lot of interest in the
upcoming pairings, including my own," said
Khon'Tor.

"I am glad to hear that. It is not good for a healthy
male to go without companionship for so long. I
certainly do not know how you have managed it.
And I do not need to remind you of your obligation
as Leader to produce an heir to your leadership."

"I know you are aware that my union with
Hakani was not beneficial. My concern that I might

find myself in a similar union has certainly played a part, Overseer," he explained.

"We have a large number of pairings to consider this time, Khon'Tor. As you know, not everyone will be matched, and I have no doubt you will be able to select a mate from those who are not paired. Especially with the outer communities participating this year," Kurak'Kahn pointed out.

"I am sure it seems peculiar that as a Leader you have to choose last. But I know you understand how difficult it is to match the candidates, and that the diversity of the pairs is of the utmost importance."

Khon'Tor did. He would have preferred it otherwise, but he knew that they had to spread their attributes wisely.

The High Council members would make most of their decisions in the weeks before the celebration. In the few days leading up to the announcement, any last-minute changes or additions would also be considered.

Kurak'Kahn went on to let Khon'Tor know that the Leaders of the attending communities, including the outlying ones, would be attending along with their candidates, and that during the three days a meeting would be held between the High Council members and all the Leaders of the People.

"A High Council meeting? Do Chief Ogima Adoeete and Is'Taqa of the Brothers also need to attend?" asked Khon'Tor.

Generally, the High Council meetings involved

the Leaders from all the neighboring tribes, Sasquatch or Brother.

"No. This will be a meeting for the People's Leaders only. It is very important that this restriction be strictly kept."

"I understand. I will make sure of it, Overseer." Khon'Tor would make sure of it, but he certainly did not understand.

The two males bade each other farewell, and Khon'Tor continued on his way back to Kthama. With the last of the honey given to Kurak'Kahn, his satchel was almost empty except for the few items he had brought but not had occasion to use. He had spent a fair amount of time on them and was disappointed he would have to wait for another opportunity to test them out.

As he arrived home, Khon'Tor was greeted by Akule.

"I will tell you all about it—and about the females—as soon as I have rested, Akule." Khon'Tor was dusty and tired from his travels. It had been a grueling trip, though not without its rewards.

"Look for me later after the evening meal, and we can talk then. I will say this much, Akule; you cannot go wrong with any of the maidens from either the Far High Hills or the Deep Valley."

Akule was very obviously anxious to hear more,

but for the moment Khon'Tor retreated to the sanctity of his quarters.

With Hakani gone so many seasons ago, his quarters had become a place of rest and escape. Finally home, he let himself again savor his experiences with Tar'sa and Kayah. Within a few short months, Kthama would be teeming with visitors, and Khon'Tor needed to catch his rest while he could.

Back at Awenasa, Tar'sa anxiously awaited the monthly evidence that she was not with offspring. After Khon'Tor had released her, she had come directly back to her quarters and did whatever she could to eliminate his presence from her. She thought that Healers had ways of preventing seeding, but she could not tell anyone what had happened.

Instead, she had done as Khon'Tor said. When she and Knoton retired that evening, she offered herself to him, knowing he would not refuse her. Though she did not want to overdo it, she did the same the next few nights. Knoton joked that whatever had gotten into her, he was grateful for it. She laughed weakly, finding no humor in his ironic choice of words.

At the Far High Hills, Kayah was worrying for the same reason as Tar'sa, only more so. She was unpaired. She had been a maiden until Khon'Tor took her Without Her Consent. She had no one to turn to because she did not doubt that he would harm her if she told anyone—and she had also believed him when he said that no one would believe *her*. Perhaps, if she ended up seeded, she might stand a chance of them believing her—but her best route was to do as he said and mate vigorously once paired, passing the offspring off as premature if it came to that. Because both she and the male would be inexperienced, he might not realize she was not a maiden. Clearly remembering how much it had hurt, she was confident she could cry out convincingly.

The pairing ceremony was only a short time away. If she had been seeded, she would not be showing then. It might work. And there was always the chance she was not with offspring, and this whole nightmare would go away.

Urilla Wuti had sensed tension in Kayah since Khon'Tor's visit. She wanted very much to speak with the young female but did not immediately because she needed a subtle way to bring it up. One night she was finally able to do so.

The healer was about to come in from admiring the night stars when she saw Kayah leaning against an outer wall doing the same. It was a beautiful evening; peaceful and calm.

Urilla Wuti went up to the young female and

joined her. "The night sky is so beautiful. How can anyone doubt the goodness of the Great Spirit when seeing such a sight."

Kayah sighed, which was not lost on Urilla Wuti.

"You seem pensive tonight. Is everything alright?" the Healer asked.

"Oh, yes. I just needed some time to think," answered Kayah.

"Think about what? Is something bothering you?" asked Urilla Wuti, sensing it had to do with the upcoming pairings.

"Do you think everything happens for a reason?"

"Well, that is a very interesting question. What do *you* think?"

"I used to think so. But now, I am not sure," replied the young female.

"Has something happened that you need to talk about?" Urilla Wuti probed a little.

"No. I just wondered if there were mistakes; if the Great Spirit allows mistakes to happen," she said.

"I do not know what you would call a mistake, Kayah, but I do know that things happen that we might not have chosen. But I also know that something good always comes out of it. It might take a while to realize, but I have never seen it fail. From something we think is to our detriment, eventually some blessing emerges," she said.

Kayah put her head on Urilla Wuti's shoulder, and the older female put her arms around her. They stood there for a while, Kayah soaking up the comfort of Urilla Wuti's motherly embrace.

Kayah was pretty much alone in the world. Her mother had died in childbirth. Her father had paired again, but because his second mate's mother was ill, they had returned to her community to live. Kayah had been old enough to make her own decision and chose to stay at the Far High Hills. In a way, it made it easier for her to think of leaving to live in her new mate's community, as her ties here were few and not that strong. Except for Urilla Wuti—she would miss the Healer a great deal.

Kayah often prayed to the Great Spirit that the mate chosen for her would be kind and gentle and understanding. She was tired of being alone, and she was anxious to start a family of her own.

Oh, how she wished she could ask Urilla Wuti about mating. But as a Healer, Urilla Wuti had no direct experience. Kayah wanted to ask what it was usually like, but without letting on that anything had happened. *Were most males like Khon'Tor? Was inflicting fear part of how they took their pleasure? Or was it usually a more mutually enjoyable experience? What else might her mate do to her?* Surely sometime between now and then someone would explain to her what to expect.

Because of how close she was feeling to Urilla Wuti at the moment, Kayah thought she would at least share some of her concerns.

"Urilla Wuti? You know I have no mother and no

family. And being in line to be paired, I wonder what I am to do? What will he expect of me? I have no idea, and I am worried I will disappoint him. And I have heard stories from some of the females—is it going to hurt?" she hesitantly offered, taking a tack that she hoped sounded like the normal questions a maiden might ask.

"Is that what has been bothering you?" Urilla Wuti had perceived that Kayah's mood had something to do with being paired, but her Healer's vow of respect for other's privacy prevented her from indiscriminately accessing the younger female's consciousness.

Urilla Wuti pondered. *Khon'Tor was almost invasive in his visual admiration of the maidens when Harak'Sar assembled them; perhaps Khon'Tor's scrutiny has stirred up fears for her. There was a chance that he would select one of them. Perhaps that had frightened her. The idea of being mated by a male as powerful as Khon'Tor could give any female pause, and Kayah was delicate by the People's standards.* It did seem to have something to do with Khon'Tor.

"Let me help put your mind at ease. Remember that before you are paired, several of the older females will meet with all of you in the Ashwea Tare. Usually, the young females meet as a group, but if you have specific questions you wish to ask in private, that can also be arranged. There is nothing to be embarrassed about. This is the next chapter in your life, and it is natural to have questions—and even fears.

"I will find out when the meeting will be so you can put some questions together in your mind if that would help?" Urilla Wuti asked.

"I am sure you also know that the males who are to be paired go through a similar process. They are also taught what to expect as well as how to please their mates and make it enjoyable for them. As a female, you have the right to refuse to mate, you know.

"There is nothing you cannot ask. If you would like, I will be glad to attend," offered the Healer.

Kayah nodded, relieved that she would get some answers before she had to face her new mate.

The next day, Urilla Wuti suggested to Harak'Sar's mate that it was time to start the Ashwea Tare for the maidens. Being Second Rank, the Healer called together the older females and made the arrangements for the meetings.

As was the custom, the females of the community created a beautiful setting. Flowers decorated the room, and colorful rocks rimmed the walls. The room was both cozy and warm, and provided a feeling of safety.

The seating was arranged in a semi-circle with elevated places for the older females to sit. The maidens could choose to sit on the floor or on the seating provided, whichever they preferred. As it was a small group, only two of the older females and Urilla Wuti were present.

Harak'Sar's mate, Habil, was one of the females chosen to speak with the young maidens. She started by putting everyone at ease, telling them there was nothing they could not ask, and that the point of the Ashwea Tare was to help answer all the questions they no doubt had about what took place between a paired couple.

"I am sure you are all excited about being paired, but I am also sure you are nervous as well. I know I was. However, I was prepared, so I not only knew what to expect, but I was assured that my first experience would not be a reflection of the experiences to follow."

The maidens looked at each other in mild alarm. *What did she mean? She was saying that their first experience would not be good?*

Habil continued, "Let me briefly explain. When a male and female mate, part of the male enters into you. Because you are maidens, it will take some force for him to complete this action. But after that first time, it should no longer hurt. It is important that you know this, or you will think that mating will always be painful."

"It's going to *hurt?*" one of the maidens blurted out, wide-eyed.

"Most likely, yes. It is just the way it is. If you would prefer, the Healer can perform a procedure beforehand, so that you will not experience that pain on your first mating. The procedure will also be painful, but you will have it behind you. However, the most important part to know is that mating should be an enjoyable and pleasurable experience for both of you. The older, experienced males of each community meet with the unpaired males and teach them ways to give you pleasure, just as we will be explaining how you can please your mate."

While the maidens were still reeling from the news that their first mating would be painful, Kayah had other questions. She already knew all too well about that part.

"Excuse me, I do not know how to ask this—but what if I do not like who they choose for me?"

Habil replied gently, "Do you mean what if you do not get along? The High Council puts a great deal into its consideration when choosing a mate for you, Kayah. It will be unlikely that you will not like him or he you—especially you, Kayah. You are a sweet female with a kind disposition. Any male would be blessed to be paired with you."

Habil's kind words touched Kayah's heart.

"No, well, maybe. But I mean, what if he is not, what if my mate is rough or—I do not know. What if, after all the coaching and preparation, I do not like it? What if it *is not* enjoyable?" She finally stammered it out.

Urilla Wuti wondered where this was coming from. Had this young female picked up an impression from Khon'Tor? Was she just perceptive, or was she perhaps a potential Healer whom everyone had overlooked? It could be serious. If Kayah had an unusually perceptive seventh sense, perhaps she should not be paired until they could evaluate her. Urilla Wuti had never seen anything like that in Kayah before, but sometimes the abilities only blossomed later, as a female offspring matured.

Habil answered Kayah. "As a female, you have the right to refuse your mate. The second of the First Laws states that we are to be revered and cherished by the People. The last of the First Laws states that no female may be taken Without Her Consent. Never Without Consent. It is to his benefit to make sure that you enjoy being mated. It is in his best interest that you want to come to him. Many males have stronger mating drives than we do, and we can forego it more easily than they can.

"That being said, however, if paired mates have different tastes in how they conduct their joining, as long as it is mutual, it is of no one's concern."

"Does that happen?" Kayah's eyes were wide with astonishment.

Habil laughed. "I should not laugh, Kayah. That is an excellent question. The answer is—well, only those couples know. Since it is between them, the rest of us can only surmise. But remember, only once in our history has a female been mated Without Her Consent."

Knowing what she knew, Kayah accepted what the Leader's mate was saying. *Who knew what was going on between the paired couples? As long as no one objected, there was no way of knowing.*

But as for the last thing Habil had said, Kayah knew for a fact it was not true. There had been a second instance of Never Without Her Consent when Khon'Tor forced himself on her.

To a great deal of blushing and giggling from the maidens, the older females answered all the questions the best they could. It was the continuation of a bond between all females that they shared what they had learned about the joys of lovemating in their own Ashwea Tare—and from the subsequent years of living with and learning from their mates. It was a time of sharing information, but also of growing closer as the maidens prepared to be initiated into the fellowship of paired females.

Kayah felt much better after the first meeting, and even more so after those that followed. She was able to put aside her fears that the experience at Khon'Tor's hands was what she could expect. And she was learning ways to please her mate. Now it was just a countdown with her body until the pairing ceremony.

Urilla Wuti was pleased that Kayah's anxiety had been dealt with. *I wish I could go with her to the High Rocks. It would also be good to see Adia and the others again and I would like to see how Nootau has developed. But I have to stay away. Adia must face on her own the storm that is coming.*

The numbers expected to attend the pairing ceremony were staggering. Acaraho sat looking blankly at the rock wall, searching for inspiration about how to manage all these visitors hospitably. The only way would be for families to double up in their living quarters, freeing some of their private spaces for others. Another option would be for paired mates without offspring temporarily to join the gender groups for the few days of the meeting. Acaraho wished he could have joined Khon'Tor on his visit with Harak'Sar and Lesharo'Mok, but the Leader had been right. Without a Third Rank, the Leader's mate, should a problem arise it would have left Adia with little formal support other than First Guard Awan.

And as it was, Khon'Tor had been gone far longer than Acaraho had anticipated.

At the first opportunity, Acaraho brought up his concerns. "Khon'Tor, with your figures and the reports from the messengers, we have a staggering turnout for the Ashwea Awhidi. The only way I can finish figuring out living arrangements is to do a test run."

"What did you have in mind?" Khon'Tor was pleased to hear that so many would be in attendance.

"I need a general meeting at which I can propose my plan—which is that families need to double-up their living quarters to free as much space as possible. If we can try this out for one night, with some preparation, of course, it will give me an idea of where we stand," he explained.

"Is there anything else we should discuss at this meeting?"

"Perhaps you can report on your visit to the People of the Deep Valley and the Far High Hills," suggested Acaraho.

"I can do that. And on another very important note, when I stopped on the way back and met with Kurak'Kahn, he informed me that all the Leaders would be coming, even those from the furthest communities. And he wants to call a special session of the High Council."

This was almost unprecedented. It had been a long time since all the People's Leaders had assembled.

"And he made it very clear that *only* the People's Leaders are to attend. Ogima Adoeete and Is'Taqa are not to be in attendance."

Now that *was* unprecedented. The two men, adversaries and counterparts, looked at each other with the same concern.

Acaraho spoke first. "I will see that it happens as they wish. As far as other general information you may wish to share, I will ask Awan and Mapiya if there is any talk that we should address with the general community. We do need to ask the High Council to hold full-scale pairing ceremonies more often. Letting it go this long has created a large number of requested pairings."

Khon'Tor nodded, and Acaraho left to consult with Mapiya and the others.

Acaraho did not understand why the High Council would wait so long between full-scale pairing ceremonies. As a result, those waiting to be paired were not just the young adults coming of age. Those before them were now mature adults and should already be producing offspring of their own for the sake of the People in general. He understood that several years between full-scale pairings would provide a wider pool for selection, but far too many years had passed since the last unions of any number had been made.

And so many pairings would also mean a shift in living arrangements. The unpaired bachelors who had come forward to be paired and who did not choose to live in the gender groups would need dedicated quarters. It was enough to keep him up at night. And Acaraho, with all the other additional stress, did not need to lose any sleep.

It was also time to start the Ashwea Tare meetings for the potential mates.

If the Great Spirit had any time management problems, this would be the moment. Nearly everyone waiting to be paired was fervently beseeching the Great Spirit for a perfect match.

Following the Ashwea Tare, Adia and Nadiwani knew they would be busy answering questions from the maidens about the timing of mating to producing offspring. Those who wanted to live in union with their mates were particularly interested; many wanted to establish a relationship with their mate before having the distraction of offspring. Those who wished to live in the gender-specific communities did not generally wish to wait and were happy to have offspring whenever they came. For the most part, the majority of the maidens were hoping for a pair-bonded relationship with their mate—and of course, it was the responsibility of the High Council to match both male and female with those who shared their lifestyle choices.

Khon'Tor called the general meeting at Acaraho's request, letting it be known that it was about the pairing celebration, lest it raise unnecessary concerns.

Khon'Tor faced the crowd and raised his left hand to speak. "Thank you for coming. As you know, I recently traveled to meet with the Leaders of the

Deep Valley and the Far High Hills. They both send you their greetings and share in your excitement for the upcoming pairings.

"I am pleased to report that we have the largest number ever of the People coming to Kthama. While this is an exciting time for everyone, it presents some challenges regarding accommodating such large numbers of guests. Acaraho?" Khon'Tor stepped back from the front as Acaraho stepped forward.

"As Khon'Tor said, we have an unprecedented number of guests coming in for the Ashwea Awhidi. This includes the High Council members who will be attending, as well as the families of the candidates. To determine what else we need to do to accommodate everyone, I need your cooperation.

"As you can imagine, there will be strains on sleeping arrangements as well as personal care. I am asking you to get together with your other family members and combine your living quarters in two nights' time. This is just a test for one night and means that for every two related families, hopefully, one living space will be freed up for guests. I realize this is an imposition on you, and I apologize because you will be turning over your private quarters to strangers. However, there is no other way to accommodate such numbers.

"In addition, anyone living in separate quarters who would be prepared to spend the three days of the ceremony in their appropriate gender community, please do so. Some of us will be coming around to check on what number and types of space are freed up during this trial run. Please leave the doors to your quarters open if you have offered yours, so we know you have done so. Once we have this information, I will have a better idea of how we are to move forward. Are there any questions?"

An unidentified voice from the audience spoke up. "How can we help you, Acaraho?"

"Thank you for asking. Anyone interested in helping, please see me, Awan, or Mapiya. The work of greeting, escorting, answering questions, cooking, bringing water up from the Mother Stream, will be staggering. Anyone who wishes to volunteer will help take the strain off those I have already assigned to some of these roles."

Acaraho looked across the crowd, allowing time for anyone else to speak if they wished. As no one did, Acaraho nodded to them and stepped backward, returning the floor to Khon'Tor.

The Leader took over again. "Just a reminder, those of the females who are to be paired, at the end of the celebration you will be expected to return with your selected mate to his community. The People from the Great Planes and the High Red Rocks are participating and there is no way of knowing ahead of time who will be paired with their males. So those of you asking to be paired must consider the possibility that you may not see your families for quite some time, if ever again, due to the great distances between us. Please make your preparations accordingly. Thank you—that is all."

Khon'Tor raised his hand, then dropped it as he stepped down from the front.

The moment Khon'Tor stepped down, the community came alive. Though they knew it was a possibility that some of their daughters could move so far away, hearing the Leader state it so matter-of-factly ended the meeting on a somber note.

The heavy feeling in the room matched Acaraho's mood. He kept wondering why Kurak'Kahn would call a special meeting involving the Leaders from all the known Sasquatch communities. Usually, Leaders did not travel to pairing ceremonies—the fact that their attendance had been specifically requested meant this was not just a matter of convenience.

Something very important was going on that would affect all the People.

CHAPTER 4

Nadiwani and Adia had done all they could to prepare. In their array they had ample supplies of every possible item they could think of.

Acaraho's trial run of the changes in living arrangements had proven very helpful. It would be tight, but with everyone's cooperation, they could make it work. Feeding everyone would deplete their food supply, but the upcoming harvest would replenish their stores. A banner year for rainfall was promising to produce a bountiful return.

The watchers whom Acaraho had posted along the travel routes were making reports of guests approaching. Some guests had already arrived at Kthama, where they were warmly greeted and shown to their quarters. The Leaders were arriving with their people. Never had the level of excitement been so high.

But there was sadness too; the young females would be leaving their homes, possibly never to return. Their mothers and the older females had done their best to prepare them. They all hoped that the excitement would become contagious once the festivities and activities began.

Adia was also struggling with her feelings. In addition to the fact that Nootau was no longer an offspring, she felt a deep foreboding about the event. A foreboding she had not experienced since she had felt compelled to deliver the Goldenseal to Ithua and discovered the infant Oh'Dar, and it rattled her. She had not shared it with Acaraho because he had enough on his mind. But if it did not lift, she would turn to Nadiwani, or even contact Urilla Wuti if need be.

Lesharo'Mok from the Deep Valley was one of the first to arrive with his complement. They had traveled underground along the Mother Stream as expected.

Adia was happy to see her father's brother. She had not seen him since the High Council ruling when she had announced her seeding. He had been kind to her throughout that ordeal and now gave her a warm embrace in greeting.

"You are as beautiful as ever, Adia. Motherhood

becomes you. Your father would be so proud," he added.

Adia was touched at the inappropriate remarks, realizing he was speaking to her as her uncle and not as a member of the High Council.

"We must spend some time together. I want to hear everything that has happened since the last time I was here."

"There is a lot to tell, Lesharo'Mok. And I look forward to it." She hugged him and then released him to those waiting to usher him, the rest of his people, and their belongings to their quarters.

Next arrived Harak'Sar, also having traveled along the Mother Stream. Khon'Tor watched his community trickle in, noticing Kayah among the maidens. She avoided his gaze. If she was with offspring, Khon'Tor could not tell. She was truly beautiful. He wished now that he had not mated her, as she was one of his favorites of those he felt were most suitable for him.

She has not told anyone what happened. And she is avoiding me. That bodes well for her. Khon'Tor had to stop his mind from wandering back as this was not the time or place for that. But he was pleased to see that she was not defying him as Hakani would have by glaring at him accusingly.

Acaraho and his males had never been so busy. There were people everywhere, coming from every direction. He was grateful for the support of the Community. Everyone who had volunteered had come through, and all in all it was going very well.

Understandably, the last to arrive were the People from the Great Pines and the High Red Rocks. They had traveled overland and preparing for their arrival had taken a great toll on Acaraho's resources.

Acaraho was told that they were almost at Kthama and went to the Great Entrance to meet them. Adia and Nadiwani were also in tow. They had heard of the communities but had never met any of the People. There would be much to share with them over the next few days.

Akule was the one who directed these latest arrivals to the concealed opening of Kthama. Including their Leader, approximately thirty or so of their members had made the trip.

Acaraho dropped his jaw when they entered.

Streaming in was a group of the largest people he had ever seen. Nearly all of them were as well-built as he was, even though he stood apart easily from the People of the High Rocks in both height and build.

He could see that Adia and Nadiwani were having the same reaction. They knew they were staring but could not help themselves. These People were magnificent, each one. The skin tones of some were darker, with a brownish tint. And their hair covering was thicker everywhere. And they had the same massive chests and muscular build as Acaraho and Khon'Tor.

Smaller members could be seen in the center of the group entering, and Acaraho was pleased to realize that the females were not as robustly built as the males. He did not want the males of his people dwarfed by the females selected for them.

The greeters went to the group and introduced themselves. One of the tallest males broke from the crowd and came over to Acaraho and the others.

"Greetings, I am Paytah'Tar, Leader of the People of the High Red Rocks."

"I am Acaraho, High Protector of the People of the High Rocks. I welcome you on behalf of our Leader, Khon'Tor." Both males exchanged a shallow bow.

"And this is our Healer, Adia, and her Helper, Nadiwani. We are at your service, Adoeete."

"I am sure we will have many matters to discuss and much to learn from each other, Commander. I look forward to it."

And with that they parted, and Paytah'Tar and his party were shown to their living arrangements. On the way, the greeters told them about the general eating times and other logistics.

Once the guests were on their way, Acaraho, Adia and Nadiwani could not help but look at each other. They were all taken aback at the size of these people. It had not occurred to them there would be such variation between the groups.

Later that evening, the People of the Great Pines arrived. Adia had turned in and was resting. Suddenly, she shot straight up in bed.

She trod around her quarters for a little bit, trying to calm down, until she could stand it no longer. She bolted out of the door and ran down the corridor to Nadiwani's quarters.

Nadiwani had also gone to bed and was rudely awakened by the pounding on her door. The sharp knock of rock on rock roused her immediately. Cranky and half asleep, she went to the door.

As she opened it, she thought, *This had better be good!*

Adia stood there, wide-eyed with alarm.

"What is it? What's the matter?"

Adia fell into her arms, pressing her face into Nadiwani's neck. Though muffled, the Helper could still make out what Adia said.

"Nimida. Nimida is here at Kthama."

Nadiwani stepped out into the corridor dragging Adia with her. She did not know if Nootau, who shared her quarters, had been awakened, and she did not want to take a chance on his overhearing them.

"What? *How do you know?*"

"I know. I know. Nimida is with whatever group just arrived."

Adia was shaking. Nadiwani knew the Healer had feared she would never see her daughter again. But now Nimida was here. The young female would have no idea that Adia was her mother, and Adia could never let her know. Adia had a million questions that Nadiwani knew would never be answered, but at least she would be able to see Nimida, perhaps talk to her, hear at first-hand what her daughter's life had been like so far.

It hit Nadiwani and Adia at about the same time. Nimida was here to be paired. There was no other reason for her presence.

Neither of them slept for the rest of the night.

Both Nadiwani and Adia were among the first to arrive for the morning meal. They took their usual place and waited for the others to trickle in. Adia had a strong seventh sense, but it was clouded when she was drowning in emotion. She could tell that her daughter was somewhere at Kthama but could not single her out.

Acaraho saw the two seated together and came over to say hello. They had been going in different directions for some time and had not had a moment to spend together.

Adia reached for Acaraho and drew him down to

sit next to her. He straddled the bench as he was wont to do, so he could face her directly without turning. It was also one of his favorite positions to tease her with, though with the drain on both of them, he did not want to add to their tension right now.

"Acaraho, she is here. Nimida is here. Somewhere. I felt her arrive last night."

"What? Then she is here to be paired. When did you sense her presence?"

"It was last night. Earlier than the time we usually turn in, though."

"The group that arrived last night was the People of the Great Pines. She must have been sent there to be raised."

They sat in silence for the next several minutes.

Adia stayed as long as she could but did not get a sense that Nimida had entered the room. She anxiously awaited her first glimpse of the young female. Would she see more of herself—or more of Khon'Tor? Nootau had clearly taken after Khon'Tor, for now only lacking his father's silver crown of hair. Adia lived in dread of that unmistakable trait appearing at any time. As long as Adia remembered, even when she came to the High Rocks as a younger Maiden, Khon'Tor had sported the striking feature.

But it made no sense for Adia to continue sitting there. The large number of visitors required that they eat in a number of sessions. She could wait there all day and not find her.

By midday, everyone expected had arrived and all were settled in.

The first day would be spent in socializing and acclimating. The meeting with the High Council had been set for the following morning. The pairings would start being announced later that day and continue through the evening. The third day would be taken up with any leftover business and more socializing. The following morning everyone would say their goodbyes before leaving—or staying—with their new mates.

There would be no rest for some time for the People of the High Rocks. There would be days of clean-up and reorganization after their visitors had left, as well as the important task of tending to the new members of their community and making them feel welcome.

Having no sense of Nimida, Adia went back to the Healer's Quarters for a break. She took up her favorite position, propped against the cool rock wall, and slowed her breathing and tried to clear her mind. After several minutes she felt herself calm down, and she reached out to make a Connection with Urilla Wuti.

No window opened, and no Connection opened up. Adia settled herself further and tried again. Nothing. She could not open a Connection with Urilla Wuti. This had never happened before. She wondered if she should try to enter the Corridor. Perhaps she would find her there.

Adia focused on opening the portal to the other world, but again, nothing. She started to panic. *Had something happened to Urilla Wuti? Or have I lost my ability to connect with her?* It was a while before Adia could calm herself enough to try again.

Finally, a small window opened. She had reached Urilla Wuti, but instead of the counsel she hoped for, Adia received only one message.

"You must walk this path alone, Adia. No one can help you with what is now in front of you. But I will be here afterward. Trust yourself. Remember your father's words. We are both with you."

And then the window closed, abruptly.

Adia remembered her father's gentle admonishment that she had to practice strengthening the other gifts of the Great Spirit, The One-Who-Is-Three. Everything was being thought into existence by the Great Mind, using the intention of the Great Will, and held together by the binding force of love, the Great Heart. She had been working on her objectivity, strengthening her reason and her connection with Great Mind. She had focused on strengthening her resolve and clarifying her intentions by deepening her connection with the Great Will—the moving force of all creation.

But would it be enough to carry her through whatever Urilla Wuti had just told her would be coming? Adia also remembered her father's warning that there would be struggles ahead, as Urilla Wuti had just reminded her.

The closing of the window between Adia and her mentor had been like a rock wall slamming down between them. When she needed Urilla Wuti the most, Adia felt utterly and terribly alone.

Urilla Wuti sat in her quarters with a heavy heart. She knew what was facing Adia and wished she could help—but could not. She had to let the younger Healer find her way through the storm that was about to break loose. It was the only way not to contaminate Adia's destiny. Any further contact between them could influence her in ways impossible to anticipate. Adia was on her own now.

As Leader of the community, Khon'Tor needed to circulate and introduce himself to make his presence known. He did not mind this, as it allowed him to look over the maidens once more. And there were others whom he had not yet met—those from the People of the High Red Rocks and the Great Pines.

Khon'Tor had not been there when the People of the High Red Rocks and the Great Pines had arrived, but Acaraho had said he would have no problem picking them out. And he was right.

The Leader was used to being the tallest and largest in the community, matched only by Acaraho. Now he was face to face with an entire group of males who were essentially his equals. As fascinating as it was, he found it somewhat intimidating. He had enjoyed the feeling that his physical stature was unique.

Fortunately, the females of those communities were not as huge as the males. He would have found that off-putting, especially since he specifically wanted a mate he could intimidate with his size. He still had not decided who he would choose, but there were several suitable candidates, and he was confident that *this* time he would be satisfied with his selection.

Khon'Tor found that simply walking through Kthama was a challenge. There were bodies everywhere.

He knew that Acaraho had also doubled and tripled the watchers and guards along the route. Luckily, the Waschini threat had not materialized as they had feared. There had been no sightings and no incidents reported by any of the People traveling above ground, or by Acaraho's watchers and guards.

It was finally time for the High Council meeting. Acaraho had selected one of the largest private rooms for the gathering. Guards stationed at specific locations ensured nothing would be overheard—not even by them.

Slowly, the Leaders filtered into the meeting room. As before with Adia's meeting, a long table had been set up at the front of the room for the High Council members. Once everyone was seated, Kurak'Kahn opened the meeting with introductions.

"Welcome, everyone. Thank you for your attendance today; I realize it was a hardship for some of you to travel this far. But when you hear what we have to share with you, I am sure you will realize why your presence here is crucial.

"On my right is Yuma'qia, and next to him is Bidzel. Neither Yuma'qia nor Bidzel attends any of the pairing celebrations. They are here at my specific request, as are each of you. I will explain their role as I proceed."

Acaraho was grateful that in his role as High Protector he was permitted to remain. Whatever was to be revealed must be of utmost importance to all the People.

The Overseer continued. "Many years ago, a number of you whom I see seated here today, attended a meeting at which we discussed the warning of the Ancients regarding Wrak-Ayya: Age of Shadows. The Ancients foretold a time of great struggle for our people. They did not provide the details, only that we would face hardship and great challenges to the survival of the People. At that meeting, we shared what we knew of the Waschini, the

White invaders who had encroached on some of our territories and some of those of our Brothers. We shared information about their cruelty and barbarism—their disregard for others and for life itself. We knew that their entrance into our lands would only bring danger and heartache to our people, as well as to the Brothers."

Kurak'Kahn moved around to the front of the table, now leaning back against it, braced by his hands behind him as he spoke.

"Also, during the time we met, we discussed the four levels of Wrak-Ayya. We hoped to invoke them over an extended period, as each level would bring greater restrictions and encumbrances to our way of life. Despite the warnings of the Ancients, I know we all hoped that we would never have to invoke any level of the Wrak-Ayya, however slight. We deemed that you, the People of the Great Pines and the High Red Rocks, would be spared for some time from the Waschini threat, due to your remote location."

Kurak'Kahn paused. The silence was deafening.

"Over the years following that meeting, we have received report after report regarding the Waschini. Each report was essentially the same regarding their soulless acts. However, trust me when I tell you that we are deeply aggrieved at what we have to share with you now."

Khon'Tor and Harak'Sar, two of the most high-strung Leaders, glared at Kurak'Kahn as they waited for him to get to the point.

"All our planning for the four levels of Wrak-Ayya has come to nothing. We were wrong in our estimates of the Waschini threat—at least in how soon it would come to pass. Despite all our preparation and their sorry actions, the danger offered so far by the Whites has been minimal."

Kurak'Kahn paused for a moment to let them collect their thoughts. "We now believe that we were entirely wrong about the nature of the Wrak-Ayya."

Everyone in the room exchanged glances.

"What Yuma'qia, Bidzel, and I are here to share with you must not leave this room. There must be no mistake about this. As Leaders, it is our responsibility to protect our people from undue hardship. And worry is one of the easiest burdens to pick up and one of the hardest to set down. We will find a way through this, no matter how difficult.

"You know it has been a long time since a full-scale pairing ceremony took place. I am sure some of you thought it an oversight on our part or an act of negligence. Let me assure you; it was neither. A great deal of study and consideration goes into selecting a male and a female for pairing. I will not bore you with the details, but please trust me that it is approached with great seriousness because of the repercussions to all the People if we do not create diversity in pairings.

"Though there are many of us, our numbers are not unlimited. There are only so many combinations possible, and our records go back only several generations. Our best projections show that, despite the involvement of the People of the Great Pines and the High Red Rocks, unless we can locate other communities of our kind, the People will be on the brink of extinction in seven generations."

Acaraho leaned harder against the rock wall behind him as Kurak'Kahn's proclamation shook him to the core. Even with the long lifespan of the People, seven generations was not much time.

Kurak'Kahn returned to sit at the table as Yuma'qia stood to speak. "We are sorry to bring you this news. We have gone over and over the pairings and we can find no error in what we have calculated. Unless we find other communities with which to breed, we will eventually experience defects and deformities in our offspring."

"Is there a solution?" asked Khon'Tor.

"We are considering several approaches," Bidzel chose his words very carefully.

Kurak'Kahn stood up again. "We currently have scouting parties out traveling as discreetly as possible to the far regions. So far, they have not encountered any of our kind or any of the Sarnonn Sasquatch."

Acaraho recognized that both Yuma'qia and Kurak'Kahn were being meticulous in their choice of words and explanation. There was more to the story than they were telling.

The Overseer continued. "We have come here to make you aware of our mistake in believing that it was the Waschini who would usher in the Age of Shadows. And we have come to ask for your help. We have limited resources. We have spared who we could in scouting for unknown communities of our people or the Sarnonn. We ask that each of you also send out small, discreet parties. We realize that it may take years for them to search and return with any information. And of course, time is of the essence.

"The pairings we have arranged for this celebration are sound. You can rest assured that the next generation of offspring will have no abnormalities. As I said, it will be several generations before we have to worry about that outcome. But now the leadership of the People must come together regularly, as we must find a solution to our problem. If we do not, the People will no longer walk Etera.

"We are now prepared to answer limited questions," and Kurak'Kahn opened the floor to the room.

Harak'Sar spoke first. "What else can be done to open up our options? What about those who are not allowed to pair? With all respect to the People of the High Rocks who are hosting us here so generously, I do not mean to bring up controversy, and I ask this in earnest. What about the Healers and the Healers' Helpers? The Second Laws forbid their pairing, but perhaps if what we face is total extinction, allowing them to produce offspring is the lesser risk?"

Khon'Tor spoke up since it was common knowledge that it was his Healer who had been seeded and produced an offspring. "There is no offense taken, Harak'Sar. It is a valid question."

The Overseer answered. "Your question is timely, Harak'Sar of the Far High Hills, and in fact, we have already considered this. And for communities in which there is both a Healer and an accomplished Helper, after considerable discussion, the High Council has decided to remove the restriction. But only one may be with offspring at any moment—so they may never be seeded at the same time."

This was an unprecedented move. Only a unanimous vote of the High Council could modify a Second Law.

Acaraho could not believe what he was hearing. This meant that he and Adia could openly be paired. And they could have offspring of their own. He could not wait to tell her. One incredibly bright spot burned in this meeting of dismal announcements. He was not going to let the rest of Kurak'Kahn's message dampen his joy. The People had survived this long; they would find a way to deal with this.

Kurak'Kahn motioned to Acaraho, who approached him. The Overseer spoke quietly. "Would it be possible for us to use this room again tomorrow morning if need be, for more discussion once the Leaders have had time to think about what we have told them?"

Acaraho answered that he would take care of it.

As he turned away, he intercepted a venomous

look from Khon'Tor. *Can he be jealous of my relationship with the Overseer?*

Kurak'Kahn returned to the front of the room. "I know this has been a lot to absorb. I suggest we meet again tomorrow after the morning meal. That will give you time to reflect on what we have told you and time to bring further questions if you have them. Thank you again for coming. Please know that we are working diligently on this problem and have been for some time. All is not yet lost."

Acaraho then moved the large stone door out of the way, and the collection of Leaders funneled out.

There were several hours before the celebration would begin with the announcement of the first pairings. Acaraho had time to find Adia and tell her the good news.

Their dreamworld trysts had allowed Acaraho and Adia to take their relationship to the level of a paired couple, but they enjoyed none of the associated social standing. In public, they had constantly to monitor and suppress their desire to touch each other—whether an embrace or a quick squeeze of the hand.

Acaraho practically flew down the tunnel to Adia's quarters and forgetting to knock, he jerked open the stone door. Adia and Nadiwani were working on calming tinctures for those who were too excited by the celebrations to sleep. They both startled as Acaraho ran into the room.

He sprinted to Adia, threw his arms around her and lifted her into the air, twirling her around.

Nadiwani's mouth hung open.

Not knowing what had happened, but seeing his joy, Adia laughed in delight. He had never acted like this, and her heart sang at whatever had made him so happy.

He put her down and then took her face in his hands and kissed her long and deep. At first she resisted, then surrendered. It was their first real-time kiss. Adia was shocked while also reeling with pleasure.

"Have you both lost your minds!" Nadiwani was never one to hold her tongue.

"Oh, Nadiwani, no! Adia, I have just come from the High Council meeting. I will not go into the reasons why; I cannot—but they are lifting the prohibition for Healers and Helpers to be paired."

Adia could not believe what he was saying. She turned to Nadiwani to see her reaction. It meant that both of them could be paired and have offspring.

They wanted to know why, but they could not ask, so Adia let herself enjoy the news. She threw her arms around Acaraho's neck, and he caught her up in another exuberant embrace.

After he put her down, she ran to her friend and embraced her. "Nadiwani! You can be paired. You can have your own offspring."

"I do not know what to think," Nadiwani said. "I have lived never considering the possibility. It is hard to believe! Are they going to make an announcement?"

"They did not say, but I expect they will have to," said Acaraho, still wallowing in happiness.

"How soon?"

"How soon will they announce it, or how soon can we be paired?" asked Acaraho, trying to understand Adia's question.

"Both!" Adia laughed, unable to stop looking at Acaraho.

She had never imagined she would have a partner at all, let alone such a partner as him. Adia had known it would be possible to be paired, but only if she stepped down as Healer. Now that had changed.

Acaraho pulled Adia to him again, oblivious to the fact that Nadiwani would be shocked again. He placed both his hands on her hips and pressed her into him, kissing her passionately. Adia wrapped herself around him in heated response.

Nadiwani blushed and had to turn away in embarrassment. "Acaraho! Adia! Please! You are not paired yet!" she blurted out.

The couple disengaged and laughed. If there had been a happier day for them, neither could remember it. Little did she know; Adia would need this joy to carry her through what was to come.

CHAPTER 5

No matter what was scheduled to happen next, Acaraho was going to hunt down the Overseer to see how he and Adia could go about being paired. Pairings were to be announced that afternoon and evening, and the High Council members were there. Who knew when they would be back. He was not going to let this opportunity slip away. He and Adia had to find Kurak'Kahn immediately.

"Saraste', we can be paired today. Do you want this?"

"Yes, yes. Whatever we have to do!" Adia was jumping up and down.

"Then let's go and find the Overseer, now."

They took off down the corridor, but as they passed the first junction, Awan saw them and shouted after Acaraho.

'Not now, Awan! It will have to wait!" he shouted back without slowing his stride.

But Awan was insistent. "Kurak'Kahn, the Overseer, is looking for you." They skidded to a halt.

"Where?"

"He said he would wait in the meeting room for a while, hoping I could find you."

The couple looked at each other, then headed for the meeting room.

Acaraho collected himself before entering the room. After all, this was the Overseer of the High Council. He left Adia just outside the door, but so Kurak'Kahn could see she was with him.

"I was expecting you two would show up before too long."

It was the first time Acaraho had ever known the Overseer to smile.

"Have her come in. We can take care of this first."

Acaraho motioned for Adia to come in.

"So much for the adage that bad news travels faster than good."

Again, making a light-hearted remark? Could he possibly be happy for us? Acaraho wondered.

"Adia, I see Acaraho has told you of our decision to allow Healers and Helpers to mate."

Adia seemed afraid to speak, lest the bubble burst. She nodded.

"Well, it is true. And I think it would be fitting if you two were the first to take advantage of the revised Second Law."

"Is it law? The law has already been changed?"

"It had to be changed, Adia. This is not an arbitrary decision that we made hastily. It has been under discussion for some time. The Second Law has been changed under our authority. We were going to announce it at the celebration tonight, during the second round of pairings."

Acaraho spoke up. "Kurak'Kahn, can we be paired while you are here? I doubt there will be another Ashwea Awhidi any time soon."

"We have always allowed for a couple to ask to be paired with each other. Usually, we take time to consider each request as we would any other. But I know the background of each of you, and considering how well we all know you both, I will grant your request on my authority."

Acaraho and Adia could not help but turn to look at each other.

"I trust this will be well received within your community. I would hate to start a brawl."

Another attempt at humor—what is going on? wondered Acaraho.

"I can see by your reaction that you do not understand why I am making jokes, considering the rest of the message we brought to the leadership. But after everything you have been through, I think a little lighthearted joy is appropriate. There will be enough hard days ahead; let us grab happiness where we can.

"You have seen pairings before. After I make the

announcement, you will know when it is your cue; just come to the front together. Let us start with your union as I think it will bring happiness to all the People of the High Rocks. After all, this *is* a time of celebration."

As Adia fidgeted with excitement, it dawned on Acaraho that Kurak'Kahn had asked to talk to him. "Kurak'Kahn, I am sorry. You wanted to talk to me about something else?"

"I wanted to talk to you about your pairing with Adia. But I also wanted to say that you should share with her the rest of what we discussed today. Adia's role is crucial in all of this. She must know what we are facing as a people. All the Healers must; I do not know why we did not consider this earlier. It was a tremendous oversight on our part not to include the Healers in the meeting today. When we meet again tomorrow, please bring her with you."

Acaraho found it peculiar that Kurak'Kahn was talking about Adia in the third person. He was clearly fatigued.

Khon'Tor had not been pleased about the High Council decision that Healers could mate. He begrudged Adia any happiness. He distracted himself with thoughts of the ceremonies to come and his plans for the night.

The Great Chamber was packed. Never had so

many of the People been assembled in one place. The conversation was nearly deafening. Spirits were at an all-time high.

Finally, Khon'Tor and Kurak'Kahn came to the front of the room, and silence descended promptly.

"Greetings, and welcome to Ashwea Awhidi!" announced Khon'Tor. The crowd cheered, and he waited for their jubilation to die down.

"It has been a long time since we have had a full pairing ceremony. I know you are all anxious to begin. But, as is customary, before we start, there are some announcements from Kurak'Kahn, Overseer of the High Council." Khon'Tor stepped back to let Kurak'Kahn have the floor.

As the High Council Overseer, Kuruk'Kahn held the highest authority over the People. When he was not serving in an official capacity, he was generally approachable and personable. And during those times, most people readily liked and accepted him as a result.

He spoke. "I am honored to be here and pleased to see how many are in attendance. It has been a long time since the last Ashwea Awhidi. No doubt you are anxious to get started."

A chuckle rolled through the crowd, a release of tension.

"Before we start with what you are really here for, I want to bring you news of a change to one of the Second Laws."

Murmur, murmur, murmur.

"As you know, the First and Second Laws were established by the Ancients for the well-being and continuation of the People. There has never been a change to any of the First Laws. But the Second Laws have been modified before. Now it has come time to make another adjustment. I will not go into the reasoning for this but want you to know that it was not come to lightly or without much discussion. Trust us that we have only the best interests of our people in mind.

"The fifth of the Second Laws speaks to the prohibition of the Healer or Healer's Helpers from pairing. This law was put in place to prevent the loss of a Healer or Helper through the dangers and risks of carrying and bearing offspring. This law has been rescinded as it stands. Healers and Healer's Helpers will now be allowed to pair, with the restriction that within a community only one may be with offspring at a time—to reduce the possibility of losing both through the risks I have just stated."

Heads turned as people looked at each other, partly in disbelief, mostly wondering about the reason for the change.

"Though this change does not directly affect most of you, it does from the standpoint that when paired, Healers will have the responsibilities of their partnership and any resulting offspring. These roles will cause additional draws on their resources and their attention. To that point, we are recommending that each community must have two Helpers instead of one wherever practical and as soon as feasible.

"Change has always been difficult for us. But we must become more adaptive if we are to continue to flourish."

Most of the members of other communities did not know what to think, but for the People of the High Rocks, there was only one thing on their mind —the Healer and the High Protector!

"With that, we will start the ceremonies."

Setting aside their confusion, the crowd again responded with smiles.

All High Council members started weaving their way to the front to stand with Kurak'Kahn as part of the blessing of the unions.

Adia was having trouble breathing. Nadiwani and Nootau were standing along the wall in their usual location. Nadiwani had told Nootau the good news, which was largely lost on him as he already thought of his mother and father as paired. He was nervous for his own pairing to be announced.

"In keeping with the change to the Second Law, our first pairing will be that of Acaraho, High Protector of the People of the High Rocks, and Adia, Healer of the People of the High Rocks," proclaimed the Overseer.

A deafening cheer rose up from the crowd. Everyone from the High Rocks community was elated. Mapiya, Haiwee, and Pakuna were hugging each other with glee. Acaraho and Adia walked to the front of the room amid smiles and heartfelt congratulations.

They stood and faced Kurak'Kahn, and he took a hand of each in his. He then joined their hands together, and they faced each other. At that moment, he raised his hand and pronounced two words very loudly. Ashwea Awhidi! And again, that part of the crowd made up of the People of the High Rocks broke into laughter, cheers, and smiles, and many jumped to their feet.

Acaraho and Adia were officially paired. Tears of joy rolled down Adia's cheeks, and Acaraho set aside his official decorum and caught her up in his arms as he had done just a little earlier, and to the crowd's delight, twirled her around. He then set her down and kissed her. The crowd went wild, and cheers and hoots broke out everywhere.

The room was bright with riotous celebration. Kurak'Kahn and the other Leaders had never seen anything like it. Even those from the outer communities who did not know the story of Acaraho and Adia were smiling profusely. Love was always a cause for celebration.

Kurak'Kahn waited for the commotion to die down, not wanting to quell this moment of delight.

The couple turned to face the crowd before stepping down. They took a short while to enjoy the love and acceptance showered on them by their people. All the years of pain and suffering were washed away, and only their joy in that moment remained.

Then they turned back to face each other, holding hands in public for the first time. Adia caressed Acaraho's face and whispered to him, "Will this day ever end?" to which he gave her a knowing smile, acknowledging that she was referring to their first night together in real, waking time.

As fate would have it, however, Adia's joy was to be short-lived.

"Will Nimida of the Great Pines please come forward."

In all the commotion, Adia had for a moment forgotten that Nimida was somewhere in the assembly. But the next pairing was being announced, and Nimida was the young female now being called to the front.

Adia was finding it hard to breathe. She turned to look at Nadiwani, who nodded in understanding.

Nimida was beautiful. In many ways she was the picture of her mother; there was no evidence of Khon'Tor in her anywhere. She was dwarfed by the giants of the Great Pines where she had been raised.

As Nimida took the stage, Adia grabbed Acaraho's hand. This was her daughter, Nootau's sister, the offspring that Urilla Wuti had sneaked away to safety rather than have her fate decided by the same High Council that had stood by helplessly as Hakani claimed Nootau.

Nimida took her place, standing to the left of Kurak'Kahn, anxiously waiting for him to call the name of the male who would be her mate for the rest of her life. She closed her eyes and once again beseeched the Great Spirit for the perfect union, though she knew by now it was too late. The High Council's decision had already been cast. Nothing could change it now.

Kurak'Kahn looked through the crowd for a sign from the young male selected for her as he announced the name, "Nootau of the People of the High Rocks."

The walls started tilting. Adia's head was spinning as if all the air had been sucked out of the room. Her knees buckled, and she fell to the floor.

Of all the possible combinations from the known seven communities, the High Council had unwittingly matched brother and sister to be paired.

Nadiwani, Mapiya, and Nootau rushed to Adia. Acaraho swept her up in his arms and carried her out.

Acaraho took Adia to one of the nearby meeting rooms and helped her to sit up with her back supported against the wall. Nadiwani gave her some spring water to drink and Acaraho knelt in front of her, holding one of her hands while she sipped the cool water.

Unsure what had happened, Kurak'Kahn announced a short recess. There was no way he would have the crowd's attention now, and he was worried about Adia. The excitement of the day had clearly been too much for her.

By the time he got to the room where they had taken her, Adia was more collected.

She reached out to the Overseer as he stood in the doorway. "Please, please. You cannot allow the pairing. I have to talk to you."

Kurak'Kahn was concerned, but he could imagine no reason for Adia to react as she had. He knew the crowd was waiting for the pairings to continue, but now he had to talk to her first. In the back of his mind, based on experience, he hoped with all his heart that she was not with offspring —*again*.

The Healer beckoned to Kurak'Kahn to come closer.

He sat next to her. "What is going on, Adia? Why can the two not be paired? She is the perfect match for Nootau."

"Oh, Kurak'Kahn, it would be funny if it were not so tragic. Nimida is his sister. I am sorry to have deceived you, but Nimida and Nootau are brother and sister. She was born moments after him. I had no idea I was carrying twins," she explained.

Kurak'Kahn scowled in confusion and looked to Acaraho and Nadiwani to explain more.

Nadiwani spoke first. "It is true, Overseer. None of

us knew that she was carrying twins. Nootau and Nimida are siblings and she was taken to another community soon after birth."

"Are you certain?" asked Kurak'Kahn. "There is no doubt?"

Adia shook her head.

"I can prove it, Overseer," said Nadiwani. "Before the two were separated, I made a matching mark between the first two toes of their right feet. You can check if you wish. And there is also the matter of their first Keeping Stones—Nimida should have hers here—and you can compare them, which will show the same marks for their birth and the day of their separation.

Kurak'Kahn ran his fingers through his hair. It was enough for him. He was deeply irritated at the deception, but no doubt Adia had assumed the High Council would make her give up the female as well. And now Kurak'Kahn had to find a way out of the pairing short of announcing the truth.

Adia spoke again. "I will tell Nootau to withdraw and explain it to him later. This is not the time to go into this with him. It will take him a while to understand and to forgive me for not telling him all these years that he has a sister. But I did not know where she was, until just now."

"Urilla Wuti?" asked Kurak'Kahn, surmising that it was the older Healer who had taken Nimida away to be raised in anonymity.

Adia nodded, reluctantly.

"Go and fetch Nootau," Kurak'Kahn commanded and stood up. Adia and Acaraho looked at each other and Nadiwani went to retrieve Nootau.

Nootau rushed to his mother's side.

"Mama. What is wrong? Are you alright?" He clasped her hands in his and hung on tight.

"Nootau. I am so sorry to upset you. I am fine. I just need a moment," she explained.

Kurak'Kahn turned to address Nootau, "Nootau, I need to speak with you as one male to another."

Nootau looked up, first to his mother and then to his father.

Acaraho nodded and motioned with his head that he should attend to Kurak'Kahn.

Nootau stood up and faced the Overseer of the High Council. For the first time, Kurak'Kahn realized that Nootau had the same massive build as his father, Acaraho.

"For the time being, I have to ask you to withdraw your request to be paired. I cannot explain to you the reason. As a male, you will be called on to do things that you will not always have the reasons for—do you understand that?"

Kurak'Kahn, the Overseer of the High Council, was speaking to him. It did not matter if Nootau understood or not; he knew there was only one possible answer. But in truth, he did understand; his father had taught him that if he expected to have authority, he must respect it in another.

"Yes. I understand, Overseer."

"Good. Now we need to go back into the assembly. I will announce that due to unforeseen personal circumstances, you have withdrawn your request to be paired at this time. The people will understand, considering that your mother has just collapsed in front of them."

"What about the female?" asked Nootau.

"Yes, that is a problem. The High Council will have to deal with her pairing at another time. I am sorry for that, as I am sure she will be disappointed." Kurak'Kahn sighed.

"There is no way to make this easy, Nootau. We are all concerned about how this will affect her. I will talk to her as soon as I can," volunteered Nadiwani.

Left behind in the huge assembly room, Khon'Tor had seen Kurak'Kahn follow Acaraho and the others. Once again, the familiar relationship that was growing between his High Protector and the High Council Overseer triggered his jealousy. And as for the pairing of Adia and Acaraho, Khon'Tor had done his best to feign happiness for them but had failed miserably. The sour, twisted smile on his face as he watched the new couple return to their places had not gone unnoticed by Nadiwani or anyone else paying attention.

○

Finally, Kurak'Kahn returned to the assembly, taking his place at the front of the room. Nimida had returned to her seat, clearly unsure of what to do with herself.

Kurak'Kahn motioned for the Leaders to return to the front.

"Thank you for your forbearance with the interruption. Adia is recovering in another room. However, we will not be able to continue with the pairing of Nootau and Nimida. Nootau has withdrawn his request to be paired at this time."

Everyone whispered and assumed it was out of his concern for his mother, who had just collapsed.

They quickly moved along to the next pairing.

Nimida was sitting in the crowd, unsure of what had just happened, other than that she had come all this way to *not* be paired!

○

After several more pairings, they took a break again. Acaraho had taken Adia back to her quarters and taking advantage of the break, Nadiwani went to check on Nimida.

A female of the Great Pines was sitting next to

Nimida when she approached, but made no introduction, so Nadiwani introduced herself. Then she continued, "Nimida, I wanted to check on you as I know you are probably confused right now."

"Yes, thank you, I am. I have come all this way, and now I do not know what is going on. Will someone else be chosen for me?" she asked politely.

"I am not sure, but I will try to find out." Then Nadiwani sat down and looked directly at Nimida to make sure that the young female understood her. "You do know that this has nothing to do with you, correct? You are a beautiful young female. Any male here would give his right arm to be paired with you. I want you to know that. I do not want you to have even the slightest thought that Nootau's withdrawing was a rejection of you in any way."

The young female nodded. Nadiwani was relieved to sense that she did indeed understand.

"In the meantime, please know that you can come to me for help or to have someone to talk to." Nadiwani gave Nimida a light hug and left her to her people.

❂

The pairings resumed, and after a while, Kurak'Kahn asked Kayah of the Far High Hills to come forward. As she stepped up to the front, she made certain to avoid any eye contact with Khon'Tor.

Kayah was relieved that she was about to be

paired. The months leading up to the Ashwea Awhidi had been stressful. Luckily, she had not been seeded by Khon'Tor's attack. Soon the nightmare would be over, and she would start a new life, able to put all of that behind her.

Kurak'Kahn then said, "Akule of the People of the High Rocks."

Akule quickly came up to the front and took his place next to Kayah, trying to focus as Kurak'Kahn announced Ashwea Awhidi over them. From his seat, Khon'Tor focused his will on remaining stone-faced.

Kayah tried to hide her panic. She was not unhappy with Akule; she trusted the High Council's ability to make a match for her, and he was certainly attractive enough. And he had kind eyes. But she did *not* want to join the community of the High Rocks where her rapist was the Leader! But it was done, and there was no backing out now.

After Ashwea Awhidi was announced, the new couple left together to start their introductions. Kayah did her best to put her concerns out of her mind; she did not want Akule to think her unhappiness was related to the High Council's selection of him to be her mate.

As each maiden had been called up, Akule had thought, *Is this her?* Though he was more concerned about the match in temperament and lifestyle choices, he was pleased that most of the young females were also attractive.

And he was happy with the choice of his mate. She seemed to be mild-tempered, and she was pretty. His heart pounded with the thought of their first night together. He had no intention of mating her immediately—he wanted her to come to him—but the idea of spending time alone with her, even talking together, was exciting enough for now.

It was time for the evening meal, and everyone was adjourned until the food could be set out.

Akule and Kayah remained, sitting together as most of the others cleared out.

"Hello, Kayah, this feels peculiar, doesn't it? I am sure it must be hard for you, as you will be leaving your community to join ours." Akule spoke gently, trying to put her at ease.

He seems kind. I hope he will not rush me, thought Kayah. *And I hope he does not realize I am not a maiden when our first time comes. If he questions it, I will tell him the Healer performed a procedure to make the first time easier for me, as Urilla Wuti explained.* He would have no way of checking up on her story. She hated to start their life together with a lie, but Khon'Tor had left her little choice.

As if reading her mind, Akule continued, "I do not know how to say this, so let me just say it. I have waited a long time to be paired. You can see I am not a young male. For many years I did not want to take a mate, but then from watching others in our community, I came to realize that I wanted someone to spend my life with. I have spent many nights waiting for you. But I am not expecting you to accept me right away. We need to get to know each other. But I do hope it will not be long before you come to me. I promise I will be gentle with you, always."

He was so gently spoken and compassionate that Kayah started to feel better about the situation. She had been apart from her family so long that she had learned to make the best of things and to accept what was without railing against the difficulties of life.

From just this little bit he has said, I do not believe he would let anything happen to me, even though Khon'Tor is the Leader here.

"After the evening meal, if you like I will show you our quarters so you can begin getting settled. Then we can come back here for the rest of the announcements."

"Thank you, Akule. I appreciate your kindness." *Perhaps it is good that he is older than I am. He is already a skilled hunter and provider, no doubt.* Kayah continued to look for reasons to offset her uneasiness about Khon'Tor and make peace with her new life here.

Akule spent the mealtime asking Kayah casual questions to try to put her at ease. After they finished eating, Akule led her to their quarters, pointing out the directions along the way.

He had done his best to prepare the place for his new mate. He had asked Mapiya and Haiwee for suggestions on how to make the space more welcoming. They helped him by bringing in items the females particularly enjoyed—flowers and scented herbs, shells, and dried hanging vines for decoration. Geodes in harmony with peace and contentment were placed about. They had made him a customary sleeping mat—larger and softer, and filled with sweet-smelling lavender and rose petals. They also suggested he make room in the personal care area for any items of her own she might have brought.

Akule opened the door and let Kayah enter first. She looked around and smiled, then turned back to him and thanked him. She walked around, tentatively touching things here and there. When she got to the sleeping area, she froze at seeing the oversized and generously overstuffed sleeping mat.

"Would you like to rest here awhile? By yourself, I mean. I can come and fetch you before the evening festivities start."

Kayah was exhausted and would like nothing more than to be left alone for a while. Perhaps forever. "Would it be too much to ask—" she stopped. She could not help it; she started to weep.

"What? Please tell me."

"Would it be too much to ask for you to give me time? I am not ready to be with you in that way."

Akule was disappointed, although he was prepared for this. He had waited so long. He had such hopes for what the night might hold. But he refocused on the ultimate goal. He knew what he wanted. He wanted the tenderness Acaraho and Adia shared. But he also wanted the heated passion between Khon'Tor and Hakani that he had witnessed the night he told Khon'Tor that Adia had left Kthama.

He was prepared to wait until she was ready. The older males had explained to them during the Ashwea Tare that not all females would be anxious to mate right away. However long it took to inflame her desire for him—whatever it took to bring her to the point where she would be begging for him to take her—he was committed for the long run.

"I understand," he said. "However long it takes. If it would help, I can have another mat brought in. We do not need to share a sleeping space until you are ready. And as for anything else, that can wait too."

Kayah was grateful for his response. She had nowhere to go; all she had was Akule. *He is gracious now, but how long will his patience hold out? I may never be ready to mate. And what then?*

Akule was good to his word, he left and only returned several hours later with a second mat that he placed as far away from hers as possible.

When Nimida was called to the front, Khon'Tor had been transfixed. He had not noticed her before, but then realized he would not have as she was from the People of the Great Pines, a community located a great distance from the High Rocks. He could not take his eyes off her and felt a tremendous regret that she was being paired with someone. She would have been his First Choice if he'd had the opportunity. From the tips of her toes to the top of her head she was a prize of great value. He was shocked when Kurak'Kahn returned and announced she would not be paired to Nootau.

The evening meal came and went. Khon'Tor was growing impatient. He had thought the situation over and come to a decision. Nearly panicked over the idea of not securing her now that he had his chance, he needed to talk to Kurak'Kahn, *immediately.*

He found him still in the eating area, sitting with Acaraho and Adia. "May I speak with you, Overseer?" he asked, nodding to Acaraho, but once again ignoring Adia completely.

"Of course, Khon'Tor. May I ask what you wish to speak about?"

Khon'Tor looked at Acaraho and then back to Kurak'Kahn. He did not want to speak in front of the High Protector, but then decided it was of no matter. He was within his rights, but he did not know what had taken place over Nootau's pairing with the female, and he did not want to miss his chance if she was available as he understood—nor risk claiming her in front of everyone if some undisclosed problem had surfaced.

The Leader straddled the bench and squeezed in front of Adia, facing Kurak'Kahn. He was now sitting with his back to Adia, blocking her completely. He had no compunction about being openly rude to her.

Adia sighed.

"I will be announcing my choice of mate tonight. I thought you should know whom I have chosen." It was out of the ordinary and not necessary, but Khon'Tor was determined.

"I choose Nimida of the People of the Great Pines."

○

Adia and Acaraho both almost fell off their seats.

Kurak'Kahn hesitated before answering, wondering if either Acaraho or Adia could find a platform from which to object. If they did not speak up soon, he would have no recourse except to acknowledge Khon'Tor's choice. No matter how uncomfortable it might be for Adia that her daughter was Khon'Tor's mate, Kurak'Kahn had no grounds to deny Khon'Tor his choice.

He waited.

○

Adia could take it no longer. All the years of coverups, lies of omission, protecting Khon'Tor, allowing Acaraho to take the blame for her seeding, the hardship Khon'Tor had brought down on her because of Oh' 'Dar; all of it came to a head. Something in Adia broke.

It has to stop, and it has to stop now.

"I call for the High Council." Adia stood up and stepped away from the table, forcing Khon'Tor to turn and acknowledge her proclamation.

"On what basis?" Khon'Tor jumped to his feet, spinning to face her. "Nootau withdrew his request to mate. The female is available."

He slammed his fist down on the table. "It is my *right to choose!*"

Everyone left in the room turned to look.

"I call for the High Council! That is *my* right!" she shouted.

"On what basis?" repeated Khon'Tor, leaning in toward Adia. The acoustics of the Great Chamber amplified their raised voices.

Acaraho had also had enough. Suddenly, he leaped over the top of the table and landed directly between Khon'Tor and Adia. He planted his palm squarely in the middle of Khon'Tor's chest, holding the Leader where he stood.

Khon'Tor looked down at Acaraho's hand and looked back up at him with narrowed eyes. His lip curled, revealing his sharp canines. All attention was focused on the two adversaries, about to take each other apart in front of everyone.

"Enough!" Kurak'Kahn slammed down his fist. 'The Healer has called for a High Council hearing. It is her right. She does not have to give a reason. Khon'Tor, it *is* your right to choose a mate, but since the Healer objects to your choice, we will hear her reason before you can claim the female. If her reason lacks sufficient merit, you will be allowed to continue with your choice.

"We will convene first thing in the morning. We will have to postpone the other morning activities," Kurak'Kahn continued, with a sigh.

By now, several of Acaraho's guards had come over and were loyally standing by, in case they were needed.

Acaraho removed his hand from Khon'Tor's chest without breaking eye contact but kept his body squarely between the Leader and Adia.

"We will need the two Chiefs from the Brothers," Kurak'Kahn added.

Acaraho raised a hand, and his First Guard, Awan, stepped forward. Without taking his eyes off Khon'Tor, Acaraho said, "Awan, dispatch two males to the Brothers. Explain to them that there is an emergency High Council meeting tomorrow morning that requires their participation. Have the guards wait and escort Chief Ogima Adoeete and Second Chief Is'Taqa back to Kthama with my sincere apologies for the short notice. Please explain that their attendance is critical to the matter at hand." Acaraho's eyes never left Khon'Tor's.

The First Guard nodded and left to do as Acaraho had ordered.

The room had completely quieted when Khon'Tor raised his voice for the first time, and talk had not resumed.

Kurak'Kahn's voice resounded with authority. "Now we will disband. Khon'Tor, you go in one direction and Acaraho and Adia, go in another. If there is any contact between the two parties before the High Council meeting, I will bring disciplinary counts against all of you."

Khon'Tor turned to leave but not without throwing Acaraho one more brutal look. Acaraho steeled his eyes as if daring Khon'Tor to read his mind.

Kurak'Kahn shook his head. As Acaraho and Adia turned to leave, the Overseer whispered to Adia, "This had better be good."

Adia rolled her eyes and said, just under her breath, "Oh Kurak'Kahn, hang onto your seat."

Acaraho and Adia walked back to her quarters in silence, neither saying a word until they could speak in private.

Acaraho could not fault Adia for what she had done. It was strategically the best move possible.

Khon'Tor was within his rights to choose Nimida because Nootau had stepped aside, releasing her into the pool of candidates. Adia only had so many options to try to block Khon'Tor's choice.

Once inside, Adia paced. She picked up a cornflower bloom and started plucking it to pieces. "Of all the Maidens to pick—"

"It was quick thinking on your part to call for a High Council hearing. But what are you going to use as the basis for your objection?"

"I will have to reveal to the rest of the Council that Nimida and Nootau are brother and sister and hope that the history of animosity between Khon'Tor and me will prove to be enough to block the pairing. Kurak'Kahn already knows I hid the fact that there was a second offspring. I am sure he will be expecting that as my argument. Perhaps I can also block it based on her being the daughter of a Healer, possibly with her own potential in that regard—I am not sure. It is uncharted ground."

Acaraho came and put his hands on Adia's shoulders. "Our whole life is built on uncharted ground." He paused. "There is one sure way to block it, Adia," he whispered.

Adia slowly let out a sigh.

She had kept the secret of Khon'Tor's attack on her for all these years. She had done so to protect the community from sure destruction as a result of the civil unrest that would ensue. It was her word against his. Everyone assumed that Nootau was Acaraho's, and that assumption had been acted out when Acaraho stepped up to mentor both Nootau and Oh'Dar. It was clear that their relationship was close, and the community had been gracious and generous in accepting them despite their obvious fall from grace with Adia's seeding.

After all these years, is our community perhaps strong enough to accept such an accusation? Could my word be enough to bring Khon'Tor down—the most respected Leader of all the People? After all this time, is it even right to do so? But this is Nimida's life, and to protect her, I will do what I have to.

"Only as a last resort, Acaraho. Only as the ultimate last resort.

"And what about Nimida? What is she feeling now? And how are we going to break this to Nootau? Oh, everything is such a mess." Adia threw her arms around Acaraho, and what was left of the cornflower petals floated to the ground.

"Not much of a first night together, is it my love? I am so sorry," she apologized.

"We have the rest of our lives together. That is all that matters. Do you want to return for the rest of the pairings?"

There were still more to be announced that evening.

"Oh, I do not think we will be missed. It would be

unfair for us to attend after the spectacle we created earlier. We need to let the new couples have the floor. And Khon'Tor will have to be there. Kurak'Kahn was clear that he did not want the three of us anywhere near each other."

Acaraho agreed, "Where would you like to spend our first night together?" he asked. "Your quarters or mine?"

It was not until then that they became aware that the Healer's Quarters had been decorated while they were away. Apparently, Nadiwani had been busy; she had given Adia's quarters the same treatment as Akule's had received.

Beautiful fresh and dried flowers, colorful rocks, and hanging fresh herbs were everywhere. And in the sleeping area was the largest, fluffiest sleeping mat ever. They laughed when they looked around and saw everything they had missed.

"Well, I guess we are staying here, yes?" Adia laughed.

"Do not worry; I will not try anything. I do not want to spend our first *real* night together competing for your attention."

Adia smiled and just shook her head.

Acaraho kept his word. The two cuddled up together on the puffy, sweet-smelling bed, and slept away their first night together as a paired couple.

CHAPTER 6

As Leader, Khon'Tor had to attend the evening announcements. He was glad to see that neither Acaraho nor Adia was there.

The rest of the pairings were uneventful. Each of the paired couples looked like they would go well together. Everyone seemed pleased with their matches. The High Council may have taken a long time between pairings, but they had done a great job.

Nadiwani and Nootau were in attendance, though with no idea where Adia and Acaraho were. They had arrived late and had heard none of what had taken place between Khon'Tor, Adia, and Acaraho.

Khon'Tor had a hard time keeping his mind on what was going on. Time was of the essence. He wanted this settled before the Ashwea Awhidi ended.

He wanted Nimida. She was here, within his grasp, and he did not want her leaving Kthama.

Finally, the ceremony was over. Khon'Tor wove his way through the packed mass of bodies. He could not get back to his quarters fast enough.

Once out of sight, he released his pent-up anger, storming down the corridor to his quarters. He almost split the rock door in two as he jerked it open. He pushed it closed after him and looked around the quarters for some release. He should have gone down into the Valley and uprooted some trees before the evening ceremonies. But the summer nights stayed light much later, and he would not want anyone to hear the commotion and come to investigate. He did not want anyone to see him in such a state.

Must she fight me on everything? Why would she object to my pairing with Nimida? Nootau removed his request to be paired. She cannot reserve the female forever until he makes up his mind.

The next day would be a very difficult one. Acaraho had dispatched escorts to bring the two Chiefs of the Brothers to Kthama for the meeting tomorrow. Khon'Tor knew he needed to sleep, but he was far too agitated.

He kicked his sleeping mat, sending the contents flying. That provided no satisfaction, so he picked up one of the seating boulders and was about to smash it against the wall, but paused, thinking about the mess and noise it would make. As he set the boulder back down, he spotted the satchel he had taken with him to the other communities, the Deep Valley and the Far High Hills.

In his anger, he had forgotten his plans for the evening's entertainment. What better release for his anger!

Khon'Tor thought about the People of the Great Pines and the High Red Rocks. Some of the males were nearly his size, and many were his equal. At first it had bothered him, but now he saw it as an advantage.

Khon'Tor picked up the satchel and removed the few items he needed and left Kthama. He knew every trail and path around. He knew which were visible from the various vantage points of the watcher, and he knew the few that weren't. Darkness was falling, and now it was just a matter of whether luck was with him tonight or not.

Linoi was out in the perfect summer night. She had left the cave system looking for some privacy to process her feelings. It had been exciting to keep her sister company on the trip to the ceremony, but they would be going their separate ways tomorrow. Her sister had been paired with someone from the High Red Rocks, so very far away, and Linoi would be returning home.

I wonder if I will ever see her again. She walked

along one of the well-marked paths, unsure where it led but seeing that it had a lot of use. Linoi was lost in reflection, but she stopped at one point to look up at the stars overhead. They were so beautiful. Her thoughts turned to Berak. *Perhaps I should have given in and allowed him to ask that we be paired. He has been so patient with me.*

Suddenly, Linoi felt someone come up behind her. A large hand quickly covered her mouth as one of her arms was bent painfully against her back.

She struggled, but a voice said in her ear, "If you do not stop fighting me, I will make you stop. You can survive what I am going to do to you, but not if you do not calm down. For what I am going to do, it does not matter to me if you are dead or alive."

Her blood ran cold and she stopped moving.

The voice said, "I am going to remove my hand. If you scream or cry out, by the time they arrive, I will be long gone, and your body will be lying at the bottom of the drop-off. Ask yourself if that is worth it. You have only a moment to decide." Linoi nodded, hoping he understood that she meant she would keep quiet.

The giant hand was slowly removed, and then both her hands were gathered together behind her.

"What are you going to do?" she whispered into the dark as he quickly lashed her wrists together.

"Sssh. I will show you in a minute. Be patient."

And then something was shoved in her mouth, and a gag tied securely in place.

"There now. That should do it. *Now* we can proceed."

Linoi's heart was pounding. She did not dare pass out. Whoever it was, he turned her around to face him. He was wearing some type of hood and she could not see his face, but he was huge. He handled her as easily as if she were a small offspring.

He took out another piece of cloth and blindfolded her. "Oh, I hate to do this; it is so much better if I can see your reactions. But it cannot be helped."

My reactions? Oh, sweet Mother above, what is he going to do?

Her captor took a moment to move both his hands freely over her, touching her where no male yet had the right. She pulled away instinctively, and he laughed.

He then dragged Linoi a little way and positioned her up against a rock wall where the hard edges cut into her back. He pressed himself up close, so she could feel his readiness to take her. She started to cry.

"Oh, please do not cry. It is not going to be that bad. When I am done, you can go back to your family."

As he was telling her this, he ran one hand down the front of her, finally stopping to let it rest between her legs. He began exploring her with his fingers, alternating gentler movements with a harsher preview of what was to come—violating her a little farther each time until his penetration of her most intimate area was blocked.

Linoi began to sob harder now.

Another Maiden! How could I get so lucky! For a moment, Khon'Tor scared himself, worrying that in the dark he had accidentally accosted Nimida. But no, he reassured himself, Nimida was much shorter and more petite than this female, and far better endowed.

He dragged her over to a grassy spot and put her on the ground, quickly lowering himself to cover her so she could not roll away or raise her legs to block him.

Knowing she was fully blindfolded, he removed his hood so he would be able to taste her. He ran his tongue over her neck, down the front of her and across, drawing the tip of one of her tiny mounds into his mouth and teasing it. He returned his hand to its previous location.

Khon'Tor's anger at Adia drove his actions, and he pictured it was the Healer under him now, remembering how he had also taken her as a maiden.

"Now it is time for you to prepare yourself because I am about to take you. And because you are a maiden, it is going to hurt. And because you are very small, and as you can tell I am *not*, it is going to hurt even more. Remember not to cry out because our time together is almost done. I would hate to have to kill you over the matter of a few moments of pain. Try to think of it as a brief interruption to your evening plans and nothing more."

Khon'Tor pressed himself into her the shallowest amount. He felt her give way, and then there it was, the barrier he would have to force his way through to possess her fully. He realized that this was his favorite part.

"Breathe deep." And with that warning, he pressed forward hard, bracing her hips under him with both his hands to hold her in place.

To her credit, she did not make a sound, but she did arch her back in pain and clamped her thighs around him. Had her hands not been pinned under her, he had no doubt she would have tried to claw him. He could not allow that, or anything else that would leave a mark, and perhaps a clue to his identity.

Khon'Tor spent himself in her within a few strokes because the force of entry was too pleasurable. After he had fully emptied himself, he took a moment to recover.

The second time was more enjoyable than the first—for Khon'Tor. He drew his sharp teeth along her neck in between each stroke, which he quickly found out she did not enjoy because she started thrashing her head back and forth, trying to stop him. Khon'Tor had a solution to that. He bared his teeth and pressed them against her, letting her feel his sharp canines pressing into her flesh, being oh, so careful not to leave a mark. That did it. She quit fighting him and submitted. *Oh, how I love it when they surrender*, he thought as he returned to licking her neck slowly, imagining someone different.

As much as he wished it wasn't, he was aware that time was passing. He must finish up on the off chance that someone might be looking for her. Until now, he had been working a slow and relatively gentle rhythm. But it was time to go. Knowing it would only take a couple of strokes, he delivered them with great force, as deeply as he could. Had she not been gagged and frightened half to death, she would no doubt have cried out. Once again, the sweet release came as he pumped his seed into her.

Finally satisfied, Khon'Tor pulled out and rolled off her. As usual, he enjoyed the taunting afterward. "Was that so bad? Did you not enjoy it at all? Well, no matter, I certainly did. What is important now is that *you* have a decision to make. You can keep quiet about this, chalking it up to experience, or you can go inside and create a commotion, which will only result in you and the ones you love ultimately getting hurt. Seriously hurt. I can kill them all before you are even done speaking. Do you understand?"

She nodded her head in agreement.

Khon'Tor wanted to knock her unconscious while he made his escape, but he knew that this was dangerous and that it would leave a mark. Again, as with the others, it was only her word that it had happened—unless she were willing to subject herself to examination, on which he was counting she would not.

He rolled her over and untied her hands. He could not leave any of his supplies behind for fear they might be traced back to him. He pulled her to her feet and pressed her face forward into the rock wall. Dragging down some overhanging vines, he tightly retied her hands. He left enough slack that he knew she would be able to free herself once he had gotten away.

Khon'Tor replaced the hood over his face and then removed her blindfold and gag, making sure he also had them firmly in his grip before he left.

In one last display of domination, he reached around her and used both hands to pull her hips backward and hard up against himself.

❂

"*Oh, no, not again!*" thought Linoi. And then as she was bracing herself for another attack, suddenly he released her. She waited. *Was this part of the attack? Was he toying with her now?*

She was afraid to move. She held her breath, keeping as quiet as possible, trying to hear him breathing, to sense his presence. She waited a while longer, losing track of how much time had passed.

Finally, believing that he had left, Linoi wriggled her wrists, trying to free them. She realized he had intentionally left some slack so she would be able to get loose. With her hands now free, she slumped down the rock wall onto the ground. Her heart was still pounding. She knew she was giving him time to escape, but that was what she wanted.

She had no idea who he was. He had spoken in whispers, his true voice a mystery. It could have been anyone. *I have no clue, no idea who he was. He was huge, but half the males here are big. He could be anyone. He is going to get away with this, and there's nothing I can do about it.*

He had not killed her. He had not permanently physically harmed her. The last thing she wanted to do was to give him cause to come after her later—or her loved ones. Linoi shuddered, then broke down and cried. *Did he have this planned? Did he single me out for this? Or was I just unlucky?*

After a while, pulling herself together, she thought, *I need to clean myself up and find a way to pretend that none of this happened.*

She wanted never to see or hear of this place again.

Khon'Tor took another route back to Kthama. He did not want to be seen coming in from the same direction as the young female. He stopped to bury his ties and gags in a place where no one would think to look. He would come back for them another time.

Before going back, he stopped to wash up at one of the small streams leading off the Great River. He did not want to return with the scent of mating on him.

Finally, dry and composed, Khon'Tor entered Kthama. Awan was on guard, and Khon'Tor acknowledged him as he walked past. He stopped to make small talk with several of the guests on his way back to his quarters. When he arrived, he collapsed on his sleeping mat and fell soundly asleep, not allowing the return of his thoughts about Adia and her High Council hearing.

Linoi also found a small creek, and much as it hurt, washed him out of her. Then she lay down and looked up at the stars overhead while she waited to dry off. She realized that this was how the evening had started—thinking what a beautiful night it was. By the time she returned, the rest of her family was sound asleep in their guest quarters. She slipped silently into bed next to her sister for the last time. After that night, neither of their lives would ever be the same.

The next morning, the males whom Awan had sent returned with the two Chiefs of the Brothers, Ogima Adoeete the High Chief, and Is'Taqa the Second. Because of the unexpected and urgent nature of the request, they arrived on horseback. The guards traveled separately so as not to scare the ponies, and they were able to make it to Kthama while it was still early morning.

Awan stood in attendance as the two Chiefs dismounted. Ogima Adoeete removed his Chief's staff from where it was secured to his pony. Awan then assigned two guards to tend to the animals, which were none too happy about it.

Turning back to Ogima Adoeete and Is'Taqa, Awan asked them, "Have you had time to eat? Would you prefer to rest while I find out when and where you are to meet?"

Ogima Adoeete replied that they had not eaten because they had come there directly.

Awan led them to the Great Chamber. Spotting Kurak'Kahn and the males he had brought with him, Yuma'qia and Bidzel, he took the two Leaders over to sit with them.

Recognizing the Brothers' Chief and Second Chief, one of the females brought out a good assortment of fruits, berries, nuts, and roots for the two men.

Ogima Adoeete and Is'Taqa knew that whatever

they were here for could not be discussed until they were all together in an official capacity, so they prepared to make small talk.

When the two Brothers sat down, Yuma'qia and Bidzel excused themselves, saying they needed to pack up in preparation for leaving in a day or so. Kurak'Kahn surmised the real reason was that they wanted to avoid any questions about their role with the High Council as the Brothers were not to know any part of the challenges facing the future generations.

Acaraho awoke before Adia and lay there quietly, not wanting to disturb her. She needed all the rest she could get. After everything was over, they would still have to talk to Nootau and try to get him to understand why they had lied to him all these years. How would that be possible without the missing piece that Khon'Tor, and not Acaraho, was his father? There was no justifiable reason for them to have sent Nimida away if Acaraho had seeded them.

He was finally forced to wake Adia because time was slipping by. Surely by now, Ogima Adoeete and Is'Taqa had arrived, and the hearing would start soon.

Meanwhile, Nadiwani still had no idea what was going on. She only knew that for some reason, the

Brothers' Chiefs had suddenly arrived, and that Khon'Tor was even more angry than usual.

The morning meal was almost at an end.

Though Kurak'Kahn did not doubt Nadiwani's story about Nootau and Nimida, he needed to see for himself.

"You mentioned something about Nootau the other day. I need you to show me." He hoped she could pull it off casually enough.

"Oh, sure! Nootau, show Adik'Tar Kurak'Kahn your birthmark—the one between your toes!" She tried to keep it lighthearted. Nootau gave Nadiwani a look somewhere between embarrassment and total exasperation.

He went around the table and reluctantly placed his foot on the bench in front of Kurak'Kahn and showed him the tiny black mark between his first two toes. It looked like a birthmark, except, noticed Kurak'Kahn, it was unnaturally shaped.

Kurak'Kahn thanked the young male, and Nootau returned to his seat, giving Nadiwani a puzzled look. The Overseer excused himself and went to find Nimida. She was sitting toward the back with the People of her community. They sat up, attentive, as the Overseer of the High Council approached them.

"Good Morning." Kurak'Kahn stopped. He had

no idea how he was going to make this request. There was just no way to ease into it. He looked back at Nadiwani and motioned for her to join him.

"Hello, Nimida. I hope you remember me; we met yesterday." Then Nadiwani turned to address the older female who seemed to be Nimida's escort.

"May we please borrow Nimida for just a moment? It will not take long, I promise. We will have her back with you in just a few minutes."

The female shrugged and nodded, and Nimida rose to go with them. There was a small room just around the corner; the three entered, and Nadiwani closed the door behind them.

"I know this is going to seem very peculiar, but do you have any birthmarks, Nimida?" She was careful not to ask specifically if she had a mark between her toes. How would Nadiwani know that if she had never seen the young female until now?

"Well, I do not know if it is a birthmark, but I do have a peculiar mark between two of my toes. Would that count?"

"Probably. Can you show us?" Nadiwani said nonchalantly.

Nimida set her foot up on one of the seating rocks, and there, in exactly the same place, was exactly the same mark Kurak'Kahn had seen on Nootau moments before.

"Thank you, Nimida. I am sorry that we interrupted your meal. We will take you back now to your —" Nadiwani left her sentence an open-ended question, trying to find out who the traveling companion was.

"That is my mother's sister, Kinya. She came with me. She is all the family I have," Nimida explained.

"Well, thank you again," said Kurak'Kahn, and Nadiwani took the young female back to where her aunt was waiting.

The two Chiefs watched Kurak'Kahn and Nadiwani go from Nootau to Nimida. They did not know what was going on but were sure they were soon to find out.

Time was up. Acaraho and Adia headed to the meeting room where the High Council hearing would convene.

Awan came along shortly after, bringing Ogima Adoeete and Is'Taqa. Ogima Adoeete was taking longer to get around these days, Adia noticed. His Chief's staff had now become more of a walking stick than the sign of his position as High Chief.

Acaraho had staked several guards at various positions along the route to the meeting room. He had arranged a table at what might be considered the back, where the High Council would sit, and seating that faced the table for everyone else. Though he wanted to sit with Adia, in this instance Acaraho needed to maintain his position as High

Protector. He would stand to the side where he had the best view of everyone involved.

It was an official matter and was treated as such. After everyone was seated, Kurak'Kahn opened the hearing as was customary by addressing the Leader of the community in which the matter was being brought.

"Khon'Tor, Leader of the People of the High Rocks," began the Overseer.

Khon'Tor stood.

"We have been asked to consider a matter of importance to the welfare of your people. As Leader of the People of the High Rocks, I welcome your attendance. You will be able to hear all the testimony of anyone involved; however, since this involves your community directly, you will not participate in our determination of whatever action we may deem appropriate in this regard. After everyone has been heard, you will be given time to make whatever statements you wish. Do you understand and accept these protocols?"

Khon'Tor stated that he did. He was having trouble separating this hearing from the last. His anxiety was rising quickly.

Seated at the table were the same High Council members from years earlier when Adia had admitted breaking Second Law and being with offspring. Ogima Adoeete, High Chief of the Brothers, Is'Taqa, Second Chief of the Brothers and Ogima Adoeete's right hand. Then Lesharo'Mok, from the People of the Deep Valley, with whom Khon'Tor had visited on his recent travels. Because Lesharo'Mok was a blood relative of Adia, Khon'Tor did not know how objective he would be, though they each took a vow of objectivity when they became High Council members. Next to Lesharo'Mok sat Harak'Sar, Leader of the People of the Far High Hills—another with whom Khon'Tor had recently met. And of course, Kurak'Kahn the High Council Overseer himself.

Ordinarily, the person bringing the complaint would be asked to step forward, but Kurak'Kahn came around the table and addressed the other High Council members first.

"For those of you who have not been in attendance here over the past two days, for you to understand the situation I must explain what has happened. People and Leaders from many of our communities traveled here to Kthama for the Ashwea Awhidi, a celebration of pairings. You have been in attendance before, Chief Ogima Adoeete and Second Chief Is'Taqa, when pairings were announced as part of High Council meetings in the past—so you are familiar with the proceedings.

The High Council pre-arranges all the pairings except for that of a Leader. As you know, a Leader has the right to select his mate. It has been this way for as long as we can remember and is part of the Second Laws. Khon'Tor Adoeete, Leader of the People of the High Rocks, has made a selection, to which Adia Adoeete, Healer of the People of the High Rocks, has objected. Khon'Tor finds no basis for her objection and claims the young female. Adia has appealed to us to set aside his claim. This is the matter before us for consideration."

Before he returned to his seat, Kurak'Kahn addressed Khon'Tor and Adia.

"You will each be given a chance to make your case, but I will ask you now—is that a fair and accurate assumption of the *basics* of the situation?"

"Yes, Kurak'Kahn," answered Khon'Tor.

"Yes, Overseer," testified Adia.

The tension seemed to be sucking all the air out of the room.

"Before we continue, do either of you have anyone you wish to call on your behalf as part of the proceedings? If so, speak now so they can be brought here directly."

"I ask for Nadiwani, Healer's Helper of the People of the High Rocks," said Adia.

Kurak'Kahn nodded to Acaraho, who stepped briskly out of the room and sent one of the guards to find Nadiwani. Adia had known she would need her friend and Nadiwani was waiting close by to back Adia's claim that both Nootau and Nimida were her offspring, brother and sister. The guard returned with her in moments.

"Khon'Tor, I will ask that you state your case first."

Khon'Tor stood and approached the table.

"It has been many years since my mate, Hakani, died. Despite the long years since that time, I have elected not to take another mate. However, since I have a responsibility to provide an heir for my leadership, I informed the Overseer that I would be choosing a mate at this celebration. As part of the planning for this event, I visited both the People of the Deep Valley and the People of the Far High Hills. During those visits, each of the Leaders was gracious enough to let me meet the maidens who would be available for pairing. Of course, not knowing who would already be paired by the High Council, I had to wait to choose until those were announced. Still, there were several suitable candidates, and I came into the Ashwea Awhidi with high hopes of making a choice."

Khon'Tor turned to look back at Adia before continuing. "Nootau, son of Adia, the Healer, was one of our young males asking to be paired. As the pairing announcements began on the first day, following the pairing of High Protector Acaraho and the Healer Adia, a young maiden was called to the front. Nimida of the People of the Great Pines."

Both Ogima Adoeete and Is'Taqa knew they had missed something very important when Khon'Tor mentioned the pairing of Acaraho and Adia. They very much wanted to interrupt and ask for an explanation but knew they could not. If it were material to the matter before them, it would be discussed, but otherwise they would have to find out later what Khon'Tor was talking about.

"Next, Kurak'Kahn, the Overseer, called for Nootau to step forward as her mate. Later, Kurak'Kahn announced that of his own accord, Nootau had rescinded his request to be paired. At that point the female, Nimida, became available. That afternoon, I approached Kurak'Kahn and informed him that I would be taking Nimida as my mate. The Healer objected, and that is why we are here."

In Kurak'Kahn's opinion, Khon'Tor had stated the facts fairly, but for the record, he turned to Adia and asked if this was a fair representation of what had happened. Adia agreed, and Kurak'Kahn told Khon'Tor to continue if he had anything else to say.

He did have. "I recognize that our Healer, Adia, has suffered many difficulties over the years. No doubt, the idea of her only son taking a mate is a difficult time for a mother. I can only imagine the strain she has been under. However, Nootau voluntarily gave up his claim to Nimida. There is no provision for him or his mother to keep her in reserve on the off chance that he should change his mind later. I have been alone for many years, High Council. Though I can understand their position, I am within my rights to claim Nimida."

"Do you wish to add anything else, Khon'Tor?" asked the Overseer.

"Not at this time, Overseer." Khon'Tor returned to his seat.

Kurak'Kahn paused to reflect on Khon'Tor's statement. *He stated his case well. On its merits there truly is no basis for Adia's objection. The fact that there is animosity between her and Khon'Tor does not diminish his rights. Not any more than Hakani's animosity toward Adia prevented the High Council from setting aside her right to claim Nootau so many years ago. Heart-wrenching decisions are often unavoidable based on the facts and laws alone, even though the High Council might prefer to hand down a different decision.*

Kurak'Kahn continued with the hearing.

"Adia, Healer of the People of the High Rocks, please step forward and state your case."

Adia was not as composed as she wished. She had not spent time as she should have in preparatory meditation. Everything had happened so fast. She appealed now to the Great Mother that her words would carry enough weight to sway their decision in her favor.

"High Council members and Overseer; many years ago, I stood before you and confessed that I had broken the Second Law and was with offspring. At that time, I asked that you remember my commitment to my calling as Healer and my love and dedication to my people. I asked for your mercy and not your judgment, knowing that you had every right to condemn me for my failings. Never did I expect that so many years later, I would once again be standing here before you, asking you to vacate a seemingly valid claim on the basis of mercy and not justice."

Even while she was speaking, she could see that the High Council members did not understand where she was going. All except Kurak'Kahn, who knew that Nimida and Nootau were brother and sister. He knew she was going to appeal to the High Council to set aside Khon'Tor's claim because of the Leader's continued animosity toward her.

"At the end of my testimony, you ruled that I must forfeit one of my offspring—either Oh'Dar the Waschini offspring I had rescued, or the one I was carrying in my womb. After your ruling, Hakani, mate of Khon'Tor, known to carry long-standing animosity toward me, claimed whichever offspring I would give up. At the time, the High Council stated that she was within her rights to claim the offspring and that it had no authority to set aside her claim. In the end, I chose to give up the offspring I was carrying, because without a doubt in my mind, to give up the Waschini was to condemn him to death at Hakani's hands.

"The outcome of that situation was that Hakani abducted Nootau, my offspring who had been turned over to her, intending to take him with her to her death. Only my intervention and that of Acaraho,

High Protector of the People, prevented him from being murdered at Hakani's hand.

"Khon'Tor and I have never had an easy relationship. We have enjoyed some brief periods of comparative peace, but in the background, there has always been an element of contention. I am sorry to say that on some level, our community has been disadvantaged by the tension between us."

Adia wondered if she were babbling at this point. She pressed forward. "At the time that I asked for your intervention because I was with offspring, there were facts of which I did not know. Had I known, I give you my word on my father's name that I would have told you. It was never my intention to deceive you about the facts of my being with offspring."

Everyone was listening intently. Khon'Tor looked confused.

"Part of your provision for my welfare was to provide a Healer to come and attend to me well before the delivery, and for that, I thank you. When I delivered my son Nootau, Khon'Tor and his mate Hakani were notified that my offspring had been born and would be turned over to them as soon as he was old enough.

"What you do not know, and only a handful of people do, was that I was carrying not one offspring, but two."

Dead silence.

"After I delivered Nootau, the Helper you had sent informed me that there was another offspring.

After she was born, that offspring was taken from me to be raised in safety within another community. I was never told where she was taken, and through the years was only aware that she was safe and healthy.

"That offspring is Nimida of the People of the Great Pines. The young female that Khon'Tor claims for his mate is my daughter, sister to Nootau."

She paused. "Nootau's pairing claim to Nimida was withdrawn because Nootau and Nimida are brother and sister."

Khon'Tor's mouth opened. *So Adia had two offspring. And of all the possible pairings through all the communities, the High Council selected Nootau's sister to be his mate? Of all the—*

And then it hit him.

Khon'Tor's blood almost stopped circulating. A cold chill passed from the top of his head down through his core and passed out through his feet into the floor. *The High Council selected Nootau's sister as his mate. And when Nootau withdrew, it opened the door and I claimed her. Now I am before the High Council fighting for the right to take my own daughter for my mate.*

Khon'Tor did not want to be paired with his daughter—as twisted as his aberrations might be, and as beautiful as she was, even that would be beyond the pale. He cursed himself for making such a strong case for his right to choose. *If I had looked properly, I would have seen how much she looks like her mother. Is that why I fought so hard for her? Because she reminded me of Adia, my First Choice years ago? Up until I saw her, I had myself set on the little honey-colored female.*

Based on what he had heard, Khon'Tor did not believe Adia had a case based on the animosity between them—any more than the High Council had accepted her plea to set aside Hakani's claim on Nootau for the same reason. Animosity or not, the High Council did not interfere in local matters for which they had no jurisdiction. *If a miracle does not occur, I am going to be paired with my daughter.*

All forward movement had stopped.

"Adia, do you have any proof that Nimida is your daughter and sister to Nootau?" Of course, Kurak'Kahn knew that she did, but he wanted to break the trance in which the other High Council members were sitting.

"I do. I ask Nadiwani, Healer's Helper of the People of the High Rocks, please to step forward."

Nadiwani came over and stood next to Adia. She had come a long way since Khon'Tor had intimidated her over the presence of the Waschini offspring.

"Nadiwani, Healer's Helper to the People of the High Rocks, what is your testimony in this matter?"

"I was present at the time of the delivery of Adia's two offspring. The first to be born was a male, whom she named Nootau. The same young male who was selected to be paired with Nimida of the Great Pines. The offspring were under my care until the time they were removed. The male offspring was given to Hakani, mate of Khon'Tor, to be raised—based upon the ruling of the High Council that Adia had to forfeit either the Waschini or the offspring she was carrying.

"Before the offspring were separated, I made two permanent, matching marks on the inside of their toes. Those marks are still present, as you have witnessed today, Overseer."

At that point, Kurak'Kahn turned to address the other High Council members. "In preparation for this hearing, and based on the Helper's claim, I did examine both Nootau and Nimida. Considering the circumstances, I decided it would not be appropriate to bring them into this hearing to provide evidence to you directly. As she has said, both the young male and young female bear identical marks. Based on the shape and location, I can tell you that there is no possibility that it could be coincidental."

He turned back to Nadiwani. "Do you have anything else to add?"

"If you desire additional proof, I made a Keeping Stone for each of the offspring. The stones were identical. Nimida is likely to have her stone with her, and they could easily be compared. On the day they were born, and on the day they were separated, I made specific marks that each stone will reflect."

Kurak'Kahn turned to the High Council

members and asked, "Are you convinced that Nootau of the People of the High Rocks and Nimida of the People of the Deep Pines are indeed brother and sister, offspring of Adia, Healer of the People of the High Rocks?"

Each High Council member stated that yes, they accepted it as truth.

"Thank you, Nadiwani; your further testimony is not needed. You may sit down."

Kurak'Kahn was tired. He already knew that the High Council did not have the authority to set aside Khon'Tor's claim. It was no different than the situation years ago with Hakani, though they were all lucky that Hakani had not killed Nootau. Adia had been right all along in her fears of turning him over to the Leader's mate. In addition, the High Council's precaution of placing a helper with Hakani had proven ineffective. But, just as in that situation, they had no jurisdiction to set aside Khon'Tor's claim. The fact that Nimida was Adia's daughter had no bearing on his right to select her. She had asked to be paired. She was, in effect, fair game once Nootau withdrew his claim.

But Kurak'Kahn was letting his thoughts get ahead of him. There were still the other High Council members. He could not rule on his judgment alone. Perhaps one of them would come up with a miracle that could turn the matter in another direction. There was enough animosity between the Healer and the Leader without adding this fuel to the fire.

"If there is no further testimony, having heard from both sides, we will adjourn. Due to the other activities which need to take place today, I will call a brief recess while we confer on this matter. Please do not leave the general area."

Acaraho moved to open the door so they could exit. He was still in his official capacity as High Protector and could not go to Adia to comfort her.

Acaraho looked over at Khon'Tor, who was still seated. He looked terrible. Acaraho knew that the Leader now realized he had chosen his own daughter to be his mate. *At least he has the decency to look sick about it*, thought Acaraho. *The real question is, what is he going to do about it when they uphold his claim?*

Despite her best efforts, Adia, Nadiwani, and Acaraho all knew the High Council was going to rule in Khon'Tor's favor.

Adia was aware that a short recess meant they had already decided. It was no different than all those years ago when Hakani claimed her offspring. She had lost.

She had known it was a long shot, but she'd had to take it.

She wandered down the corridor and slumped to the floor, leaning up against the cool smooth rock wall. She was sick of it. She was sick of it all.

For years, Adia had protected Khon'Tor. Not for his own sake, but for the sake of the People. She had set aside her right to justice to avoid destroying their community. The First of the First Laws had governed her actions: The needs of the People come before the needs of the individual.

If she had come forward and sought justice for Khon'Tor's crime, the community would have been splintered. It was her word against his. With no proof, her accusation would have opened a rift that would never close. Adia had known that the truth she held had the power to destroy their people far more than did the Waschini threat they feared.

Years and years of keeping the truth secret. Years and years of everyone thinking Acaraho was the father and blaming him for not being strong enough to honor her role as Healer. Blaming her for the same fault. It had broken her heart to know that the People thought Acaraho to be less than the honorable male she knew him to be.

And now, here she was again. Back against the wall, faced again with the same dilemma. Speak the truth and start a civil war or keep silent. But this time, it was not just her life at stake. How could she stand by and let Nimida be paired with her father?

Adia had one last move.

It was one thing to choose to let a travesty against herself go unpunished, but she could not stand aside and let one be committed against an innocent young female. The fact that Nimida was her daughter made no difference.

CHAPTER 7

I t was time to reconvene.

The others had already re-entered the meeting room and taken their original positions and the guard came down the corridor to help Adia to her feet.

It had been a short recess.

As before, Adia was too nervous to sit, but Kurak'Kahn motioned for her to be seated anyway. Acaraho was again standing against the wall where he had an unobstructed view of everyone there.

Adia remembered this same moment, many years ago, while she waited to hear the High Council's decision regarding her seeding. At that time, the tension in the room was terrible. This time it felt different, calmer. Or perhaps it was just her. Perhaps having reached her moment of final resolve, she had found peace amid the chaos she knew she was about to bring down on all of them—herself, her family, Khon'Tor, and the People of the High Rocks.

Kurak'Kahn started. "We have been asked at your request, Adia, Healer of the People of the High Rocks, to intervene in a decision regarding the pairing of a young female whom the High Council recognizes as your daughter," he said.

"The fact of the second offspring comes as a surprise to every High Council member here. Though you were under no obligation to divulge the existence of this offspring, an alternative solution to sending it away would have been to seek our counsel in this matter. Seeing that our previous decision aggrieved you, I can understand your reluctance to involve us; however, I cannot condone it."

The Overseer walked around to the front of the table to continue. The fact that Adia had been ordered to sit made his position more prominent and hence more intimidating.

"Though a second offspring produced by the same seeding does not constitute a second violation of the law which was in force at that time prohibiting the mating of a Healer, it does not foster a sense of trust in your judgment, Adia.

"A sense of trust that you have already pushed to the limit, I might add."

Adia wanted to cry at his addition of these words. She was feeling very wronged. Wronged by Khon'-Tor, wronged by the High Council, now wronged by Kurak'Kahn personally. Everything she had done, every decision she had made, had been made for the benefit of others. At no time had she made the decision she wanted to make. Her life had consisted of duty and responsibilities to others—to her detriment.

The Overseer was still speaking. "But because there is no basis for considering the second birth a crime, and because many years ago we all agreed that there would be no judgment of you by the High Council, we have no statement on this fact other than what I have already said."

As if that was not enough, thought Adia. *As if saying your trust in me has been broken is not hurtful enough.*

"Before I declare our position regarding your request, I find it impossible to ignore the continuing travesty of this situation. When we first heard your case, we refused to impose a penalty on you because you stood before us on your own, willing to bear the penalty for your personal failing on your shoulders alone. We refused to assign blame to you because the father of the offspring, who shared equally in the guilt of your seeding, did not have the courage to show himself. And here we are again; you stand before us. Alone.

"The People of the High Rocks have stood as a shining example for the rest of the People for generations. How is it now that in a fraction of a generation, we have such dissension, animosity, and disgrace repeatedly evidenced among the leadership of this community?

"You are blessed, Adia. Your community has embraced and supported you against all the odds. Despite the fact of your abject failure to uphold the purity of the station of Healer, their forbearance and acceptance speak to their great love and respect for you. It is a dichotomy for which I have no explanation."

Adia could see that Acaraho was clenching his teeth. She knew he was coming to the end of his restraint. She knew he was angry at Kurak'Kahn's admonishment of her. He had his commission as Commander, as High Protector of the People, but he was also her mate. *Where was the line between speaking out on her behalf or standing in his role as Commander?*

"Regarding your request to set aside the Leader's claim on your daughter Nimida, otherwise known as Nimida of the Great Pines, the High Council rules that it has no jurisdiction in this matter. Despite your personal feelings, despite the disappointing, ongoing animosity between you and Khon'Tor, there is no basis for us to intervene. Nootau relinquished his right to Nimida. At that point, she became available to be chosen by Khon'Tor as his mate. His choice stands. Nimida will be paired to Khon'Tor at the adjournment of this meeting."

Adia braced for what was coming. She knew Acaraho was wondering with her if the People would survive it. But, despite their fears, she also knew that he, too, felt it was time for the truth to come out. Adia might let the injustices done to herself go unaddressed, but she would not sit by and let Nimida be paired with her own father.

Adia stood. "Kurak'Kahn—"

"Sit down, Adia. We are not done here."

Kurak'Kahn was cold, angry, and to the point. He could be personable, understanding, even kind in one moment, and so official and cold in the next. "All of this drama and anarchy, all of this could have been avoided. We are all flawed. Every one of us on this High Council understands the challenges of life. None of us expects any Leader to be perfect. But your error in judgment throughout the years of this debacle gives us all pause. And the fact that the father of your offspring still hides in the shadows and is not decent enough to step forward is beyond despicable."

Everyone saw it. Unconsciously, Kurak'Kahn looked over at Acaraho standing by the wall.

Adia could take it no longer. They all thought Acaraho was the father and the coward who had let this rain down on her shoulders alone.

"Stop. You must stop!" She flew to her feet and stepped toward the Overseer.

In his official capacity, Acaraho had no choice but to act. He came off the wall and within a flash, stood between her and the Overseer. He gently took Adia's arm and tried to lead her back to her seat, saying softly, "Adia, please."

Khon'Tor knew all *krell* was about to break loose.

In that same moment, as Acaraho was trying to convince Adia to sit back down, Khon'Tor left his seat and stepped forward, raising his arm to draw their attention and announced loudly,

"*I withdraw my claim to the female.*"

Everyone now stopped and looked at Khon'Tor. In that moment, as was his gift, Khon'Tor had managed to turn the tables and come out the hero. By renouncing his right to be paired with Nimida, he had resolved the issue. On the surface, it was the perfect solution. Problem solved. Especially for Khon'Tor, who, directly following the hearing, would officially have been joined in a mateless union with his own daughter.

Kurak'Kahn turned to Khon'Tor and said, "It is not your responsibility to step aside to resolve the situation, Khon'Tor. But we commend you for your action and for putting the welfare of the People ahead of your gain—the mark of a true Leader."

"No. *No.*" Adia could take it no longer. Hearing the Overseer praise Khon'Tor and look at Acaraho with derision was the last straw.

Kurak'Kahn clenched his teeth and glared at the Healer. "Adia, you are *out of line*. I just admonished you for your continued poor judgment, not only in allowing yourself to be seeded, but also for hiding the existence of the second offspring. And to exile your daughter to another community out of cowardice instead of coming to us for direction?

Perhaps it is time for you to consider your fitness to remain the Healer to these People!"

Acaraho snapped. Still standing by Adia, he turned to Kurak'Kahn, addressing him directly. "Overseer. *With all due respect, you do not know what you are talking about. Do not* speak to her that way. She deserves *none* of what you have said to her!"

"Acaraho. I have always held you in the highest esteem. But in this matter, I am as disappointed in you as I am in her. *Deeply.*"

Adia knew there was no doubt he was referring to the accepted belief that Acaraho had fathered Nootau. Acaraho was the coward to whom Kurak'Kahn, and the other members of the High Council, had been referring.

Even though Acaraho was in far greater physical shape than he was, Kurak'Kahn refused to be intimidated. He was not the Overseer of the High Council by accident. He stepped forward toward Acaraho until their chests were almost touching.

Eye to eye and unblinking, Kurak'Kahn shouted at Acaraho, "And you are as out of line as she is at this moment. You have no official capacity in this hearing other than as the protector of order. A role you have just miserably failed at, I might add. If you speak to me directly again, I will have you removed from the room, High Protector or not!"

Acaraho did not move.

Adia reached deep within herself. It was now or never. She steeled her mind, ready to reveal the truth she had hidden all these years, trying to protect the community she loved at her own expense.

Before she could speak, a resounding *crack* echoed throughout the room.

Everyone turned to look over to the far end of the table.

Standing up was a scowling Ogima Adoeete, High Chief of the Brothers, who had just slammed his Chief's staff into the floor, catching everyone off guard.

When the High Chief of the Brothers was holding the Chief's staff, he was speaking as an emissary of the Great Spirit. He was honor-bound to speak only words of truth. They might not be welcome words or kind words, but they would be the truth.

"This has gone on long enough. We have held our tongues, keeping our place as Leaders of the Brothers. We have honored your jurisdiction to do as you see fit for your people. I have stood by through all these years, believing that honor would return to the leadership of the People of the High Rocks. But I can see now that my faith has been misplaced and misguided."

Ogima Adoeete slowly stepped around from behind the table, standing near Khon'Tor, Acaraho, Adia, and Kurak'Kahn.

"For generation after generation, our two tribes have coexisted peacefully. We have helped each other in many ways, sharing our gifts, talents, knowledge, and resources. It has been a peaceful alliance, though it was not always the case. Knowing the dark night of our past, Is'Taqa and I have held our tongues in this matter, never wishing to return to conflict between our communities. We have kept quiet, recognizing your authority to direct your own path. But I cannot stand by and allow this travesty to continue any longer."

No one, no one, no one, except Is'Taqa, had any clue where the High Chief was going with this.

He walked over to Khon'Tor and addressed him personally. "Khon'Tor, Leader of the People of the High Rocks, I have watched you lead your people through many years. I have heard you speak eloquently and passionately about your vows to protect them, your dedication to their wellbeing, your commitment to lead them honorably through whatever challenges come. Yet, in this matter, though presented with opportunity after opportunity to right a terrible wrong, you stay silent."

Khon'Tor had no idea what Ogima Adoeete was talking about. Everyone in the room was lost along with him, except Is'Taqa.

Khon'Tor looked blankly at the Chief. "Ogima Adoeete, I have no idea what you are talking about."

"It is time for the truth, old friend. *Be* Khon'Tor, Leader of the People of the High Rocks once again.

Bring honor to yourself, to your position as Leader, no matter the consequences." The High Chief was clearly saddened by what must finally take place.

Khon'Tor shook his head, frowning, not understanding.

Ogima Adoeete waited. They all waited, only two knowing what they were waiting for.

"Khon'Tor. It is time."

Khon'Tor stepped back from the old Chief in disbelief. What did Ogima Adoeete know? And how? After all this time, how could this be happening?

Adia stepped forward and stood beside Ogima Adoeete's side. "It is over, Khon'Tor. I can keep silent no longer. The time of lies is over. It has to end here, now." And she squared off in front of the Leader.

Khon'Tor scowled at her and turned back to Chief Ogima, "You are deluded, old friend. I do not know what you are talking about."

Ogima Adoeete was truly saddened. He took a deep breath, and a shadow crossed his face. He could see that Khon'Tor was not going to take responsibility. He was passing up his last chance to make amends for the great wrong he had committed so many years ago.

But still, the Chief said, "Khon'Tor, it is not too late to redeem your soul before the Great Spirit."

Khon'Tor glanced around the room, eyes darting to the door and back.

Acaraho had seen this before. At the moment they realized there was no way out for them, males started to behave like caged animals. Khon'Tor was losing control of his reasoning. He was starting to panic. It was a dangerous state of mind in anyone, let alone this powerful beast of a male. Acaraho dared not blink. He did not like how close to Khon'Tor Adia was standing. He was estimating how long it would take him to get to the Leader should Khon'Tor make even one motion toward her. *Too long.*

So Acaraho stepped forward slowly and slipped in front of Adia, easing her directly behind him. Nadiwani, understanding his intentions, crept over and led Adia back to the wall by the door, as far away as possible from the two giants now squaring off.

Is'Taqa did the same. He led Ogima Adoeete back behind the table with the other members of the High Council.

At the moment in which Acaraho stepped in front of Adia, Khon'Tor took an offensive stance against him—feet spread, arms wide, knees slightly bent, and eyes locked on his.

The room was suddenly far too small for the number of people in it considering the size of the two behemoths now staring fiercely into each other's eyes.

Acaraho did not mind the idea of fighting Khon'-Tor. In fact, he welcomed it. *But not in this setting. Not like this. Not with others around who could be hurt—or even killed—in the fray.*

If Acaraho was going to go up against Khon'Tor, he could not afford the distraction of worrying about any others in the room—and especially not his beloved Adia.

He kept his eyes on the Leader. "What are you going to do, Khon'Tor? Fight me? Attack me? Here, now? In front of everyone? The High Council, Kurak'Kahn, the Brothers, the *females*? If I have to fight you, Khon'Tor, I will. Gladly. I am not afraid of you. And we both know this has been coming a long time. I want nothing more than to kill you here and now. But I would prefer you stand down and let our tempers cool off instead. Nothing will be gained by going at each other here."

Kurak'Kahn did not intervene. He stood, frozen. Everyone was motionless. Anyone who had been in battle knew that any movement, a word, even a sound, could tip the scales in a bloody direction. Right now, it could go either way—but if these two engaged, the situation would become deadly dangerous within seconds.

Acaraho had so many things he wanted to say to Khon'Tor. But he held himself at bay. If it started at this moment, he knew it would be a fight to the death.

The two males presented almost identical, chiseled statues, frozen in a standoff. Acaraho was waiting for even the smallest tell—the twitch of a muscle, a change in breathing, a sideways glance, anything—that would signal Khon'Tor was about to make his move.

In his peripheral vision, Acaraho could see Nadiwani and Adia near the door; he knew that the old Chief and Is'Taqa were over in the far-left front corner behind the tables with the other High Council members. He also knew that he could not get to them both if Khon'Tor turned on them instead of him.

And he knew that if he had to choose, he would sacrifice his own life and those of everyone else in the room to protect Adia.

Moments crawled by. Acaraho knew time was on his side. The panic firing through Khon'Tor's mind and clouding his judgment would subside if given time. Once the adrenaline dissipated, Khon'Tor would come to his senses and realize this was not the solution that his hyper-engaged survival instinct was currently telling him it was.

Finally, the sign for which Acaraho was waiting. Khon'Tor relaxed his shoulders slightly and took a deep breath. It was not over yet, but at least it was going in the right direction.

The tension had still not left Khon'Tor's jaws. He had moved out of kill mode but was still feeling trapped. However, his posture relaxed the smallest amount, and he straightened a bit more.

Acaraho was willing everyone in the room to remain silent, for no one to move. Whoever spoke next had to choose their words very, very carefully.

Acaraho preferred that the next person to speak be Khon'Tor himself—so he continued to wait, keeping his eyes pinned on his adversary.

Reason was returning to Khon'Tor's brain.

First, Khon'Tor realized there was no point in fighting with Acaraho. In the end, there would be only one survivor, and if it were him, he would be in grave trouble for killing Acaraho. If the High Protector killed him, well, was this worth dying over? After all, so far there had been only vague recriminations—no actual accusations had been lodged.

Words. Only words.

Khon'Tor realized that it still came down to Adia's word against his. If Nadiwani knew that Adia had been violated, it would have come up long ago. So many years had passed, everyone assumed the offspring was Acaraho's. As long as Khon'Tor did not admit to it, there would be only controversy, not fact. He was assuming this was what Adia was going to bring up—his attack on her. He had been wrong in the past, so before he made a fatal mistake and said something he should not, he must wait until the accusation was made.

No, whatever the Chief had been saying, it was only a speech about honor. *The ramblings of an old man. Nothing more. I have survived worse; I can survive this too. So far, no accusations have been lodged against me and nothing has been proven.*

Right now, confusion was Khon'Tor's best weapon, not clenched fists. He relaxed, but was aware that Acaraho took a moment longer, concerned that it could be a bluff.

"You can relax, Acaraho. I do not wish to fight you—not today, and not ever. Nothing will be gained by it except that our people will lose one of the two Leaders they have depended on so heavily over the years to guide them. And over what? We do not even know what this ruckus is about."

Khon'Tor had switched to orator mode, where he was at his best. By the door, Adia and Nadiwani looked on in amazement—he was a walking contradiction. One moment ready to kill Acaraho at anyone else's expense and the next taking on the mantle of an honorable and respectable high Leader trying to soothe a volatile situation.

He continued, "Let us all calm down and return to our seats and discuss this as mature males and females."

Kurak'Kahn looked at Khon'Tor. Khon'Tor looked at Kurak'Kahn. Kurak'Kahn looked at Acaraho. Everyone looked at each other. One moment a ferocious battle seemed about to break out, and the next they were being beseeched to behave as if nothing at all out of the ordinary had happened.

Acaraho caught the attention of Adia and Nadiwani, over by the door. He shook his head just the slightest bit, telling them to stay where they were. They knew he was not convinced it was over yet and that he wanted them as near the exit as possible.

While everyone was returning to their seats, Khon'Tor was already working out the basis for his defense, should Adia break her silence. *It was so many years ago. To bring an accusation now at this point —what would be the reason? And why hide it all these years? Where was the gain for Adia to claim that he was the father of her offspring? Had she gone to Ogima Adoeete and somehow convinced him that Acaraho was not the father? How did this benefit her?*

Every angle of doubt he could throw would muddy and weaken her accusation. He was ready. He had only to stay focused on what had been said, not what he knew had happened. He had his strategy: diffuse, distract, discredit.

Kurak'Kahn realized that there could be an issue of critical proportions somewhere, and he was tired. Exhausted. He was sure the others were as well. He could let it go on now, with Khon'Tor making his statements and whoever else would be making theirs —or he could stop it now and give it the official treatment it appeared to deserve.

"Is there a complaint being entered here?" Kurak'Kahn took back control.

"I do not hear a complaint, Overseer, only the confusion of a great Chief who perhaps deserves a much-needed rest. I have relinquished my claim on the female, Nimida; to my mind, the point of contention is resolved."

Khon'Tor is technically correct. Ogima Adoeete has not made an accusation. If there was a wrong committed against someone, that person has to bring it to us for it to be heard. Kurak'Kahn sighed. *I seriously need to consider retiring—if I live through this, that is.*

Lesharo'Mok, Leader of the People of the Deep Valley, looked over at Adia. She realized he was telling her that she needed to state a complaint if she had one. So far, she had only made a vague statement about lies. She must make it official.

Adia left her position against the door, and took only one step forward, no more, heeding Acaraho's warning to keep a distance between herself and Khon'Tor. "I call for a hearing of the High Council in a matter of great importance to the People of the High Rocks," stated Adia.

An official request having been entered, Kurak'Kahn could now continue. "In the matter brought to us earlier concerning the pairing of the young female, Nimida of the Great Pines, the Leader Khon'Tor has withdrawn his claim. On that basis, the issue is closed. Nimida is not committed to Khon'Tor and is free to return to her people or do as she otherwise pleases. This hearing is now closed."

That settled, he could officially address the next

issue. "Adia, Healer of the People of the High Rocks, the High Council acknowledges your request. We will reconvene tomorrow morning to hear your complaint. We have other matters to discuss and the Ashwea Awhidi to close tonight before we can attend to your plea."

Acaraho went across and opened the large door. He leaned out into the hallway because he wanted the other guards but did not want to leave the room with Adia still in there. His solution was to take Adia by the arm and gently lead her out and down the passage with him to find Awan. The First Guard saw them approaching and came forward.

Acaraho handed Adia over to Awan and said, "Do not leave her side. Do not let Khon'Tor within a male's height of her. If he gets closer than that, you have my permission to kill him. I will bear the consequences."

Then, not putting anything past Khon'Tor, Acaraho added, "In fact, do not let any male near her. Take no chances in the matter of her protection."

Acaraho then returned to the room. Kurak'Kahn was speaking with Ogima Adoeete and Is'Taqa because he needed them either to remain at Kthama or to return in the morning.

Acaraho stepped in and offered to find a place for them to stay the night. They accepted the hospitality.

As they finally all filed out, this time no gesture of Brotherhood was exchanged between Kurak'Kahn and Acaraho, a fact that made Khon'Tor smirk.

There was not much time between the end of the hearing and the next structured pairing session, but everyone needed a break.

Adia, Acaraho, and Nadiwani headed back to Acaraho's quarters, Awan in tow. Awan waited outside the door while the three entered to talk.

Nadiwani was terribly confused. *What was all the talk about honor by Chief Ogima?*

It was the first question she asked after they settled down.

"It is best we do not discuss it; it will be heard tomorrow morning. I am sorry, Nadiwani, but if we talk about it beforehand, it may be construed as collusion," replied Acaraho.

Nadiwani was disappointed and frustrated. All these years had something so important been kept from her? She felt a pang of rejection.

"Let us try to get some rest. We still have more festivities to get through, and we need to lift our moods. It is not fair to the others if we cannot participate and be happy for them."

Everyone agreed with Acaraho. Nadiwani went back to her own quarters, and Acaraho and Adia tried to get some rest in his.

They lay together, facing each other. There was much they wanted to say, but right now, they both needed rest more.

In what seemed like only seconds, they heard the high tone of the Call to Assembly Horn.

Adia washed her face to try and refresh herself, briefly returned to her quarters to change her wraps, and then they were off to the general assembly again.

As before, the High Council members were at the front of the room with Kurak'Kahn, and Khon'Tor the hosting Leader. Ogima Adoeete and Is'Taqa were also in the crowd, as they had no other business to attend to other than to wait for the meeting the next morning. They could find enjoyment while there because pairings were always a blessing.

Kurak'Kahn welcomed everyone back and said there were two more pairings to announce, and then they could all stay and socialize if they wished. Tomorrow would be a day of welcomings and goodbyes.

As the Overseer announced the last of the pairings, Khon'Tor was ready. He was pleased to see that he was in luck this time around, unlike the last time he was in this position so many years ago. He had been keeping track of each of the maidens. Because the pairings were not announced ahead of time, there were always some left who were not paired. Of his favorites, the one he could not stop thinking about was still available. There was something about her that had stayed with him past her physical beauty—a gentleness of spirit, perhaps. She was easy to spot with her light coloring and modesty wrappings. Looking at her, he was relieved to realize that his confusion over Nimida had cleared, and this one had regained her original place as his First Choice. *With her at my side, I will be the envy of all the males.*

Kurak'Kahn pronounced Ashwea Awhidi over the last couples. When he had finished, Khon'Tor stepped to the front.

"We are drawing the official events to a close. I hope that each of you has enjoyed your stay. Never has there been a pairing ceremony of this size, and it has been an exciting event to oversee. I know that my people have worked very diligently in providing for your care, and it has been our honor to host you. I specifically want to thank my High Protector, Acaraho, as well as Mapiya, Haiwee, First Guard Awan, and too many others to name, for their dedication in carrying off such a complicated event."

As Khon'Tor publicly thanked him, Acaraho looked at the Leader, trying to decide if he were a master manipulator, or insane.

"As we started discussing this event, even from the beginning one of my people asked if I were going to take a mate this time. Some of you know that my mate, Hakani, died many years ago. Since then, I have been alone, tending to my grief and adjusting to life as an unpaired male. However, I have a duty to provide an offspring as heir to my leadership. And I admit, I have been lonely. So I came into this Ashwea Awhidi expecting to be paired.

"Therefore, before we officially close, there is one last item to cover. As my people know, I have struggled with whether to take another mate or not. It has been many years. It is a serious life-changing decision and never one to be made lightly. All the maidens paired at this Ashwea Awhidi will make fine partners, and each of their mates should be pleased with the selection. As Leader of the People of the High Rocks, though I may choose my own mate, my choice is the last event."

Khon'Tor stepped a few feet away as he often did for emphasis. Those in his community exchanged glances, waiting to see if he was choosing or not.

"Before this celebration, I visited several of your communities. I met many fine maidens and pondered many as my First Choice. Of course, it is never assured that by the end of the Ashwea Awhidi, any of those I favored might remain unpaired. However, the Great Spirit has deeply blessed me. I am pleased to announce that I am selecting nU of the Far High Hills as my mate."

The young female, Tehya, turned to her mother, wide-eyed. Only in her wildest dreams could she imagine being chosen by someone such as the Leader Khon'Tor! She had met him when he visited their people some time ago. She remembered the evening of conversation at the table after Urilla Wuti had brought them at his request. She did not think she had made an impression on him, but obviously, she was wrong.

Unlike the pride that Hakani had felt so many years ago when she was chosen, Tehya was filled with humility, and also a tinge of fear.

Her mother nudged her to stand up and go to the front because the young female did not realize she was meant to go forward.

All eyes followed her, and Tehya looked around over the crowd as she went to the front of the room. She was praying that her trembling would not cause her to trip and fall on the way.

Tehya was a very attractive young female. Her coloring was uncommon, an unusual trait for any of the People. It made her stand out, just as Khon'Tor's silver streak did for him. Everyone was comparing them as they stood together. Khon'Tor appeared even more massive and powerful next to the smaller, delicate young female standing beside him.

The People cheered and clapped. After it died down, Khon'Tor turned to Kurak'Kahn, for him to declare them paired.

Kurak'Kahn stepped forward, took a hand of each in his, then turned and placed Tehya's hand in Khon'Tor's, and announced Ashwea Awhidi over them.

It was done.

With that being the last matter, the Overseer announced the Ashwea Awhidi closed and a round of applause, laughter, and smiles coursed through the audience.

Tehya looked up at the Leader to whom she was now paired. She was sure everyone could see how hard her heart was pounding in her chest. Her trembling hand was swallowed up in his.

He led her down into the crowd and to the back of the room. Then he turned to her and said, "Do not worry, Tehya. Everything will be fine. Put any concerns out of your head about what will happen between us tonight."

Khon'Tor knew that the maidens to be paired had gone through the Ashwea Tare, as had the young males, and so they had an understanding of what happened during mating. But he could see she was concerned about something. Khon'Tor wondered why he cared that she might be worried, but for some reason, he did.

He had wanted to wait, to plan his strategy before taking her, but he was suddenly burdened by what might happen tomorrow at Adia's hearing. He had not thought of it earlier, but this might be his last mating for a long time, if not ever. And as bland as it would have to be, he had his memories of how he frightened and took the young female last night; they would stir him up to where he could complete the act with Tehya. *She is young and no doubt very fertile, and there is always a chance I might leave some part of myself behind.*

Many came over to congratulate Khon'Tor. Tehya's mother and father hugged her and met Khon'Tor. Until now, he had only been an important figure passing through the crowds and addressing them as Leader of his people.

Khon'Tor was not one to spend much time in the company of females. His life was consumed with the matters of males. Most of his interactions with females had to do with the mundane mechanics of living. The exceptions had been Adia in her position as Healer—and his mate Hakani, a union which should have been one of mutual comfort, reassurance, and support.

But as Khon'Tor and Tehya spent the evening meal together, he found her to be surprisingly good company. Despite her nervousness, she was bright, intelligent, and did her best to engage in conversation. She seemed devoid of guile or deception. If there were hidden dark corners to her, he could not see them; she was undefended about who she was. He found himself quickly growing protective of her —a sensitive soul in a world fully capable of taking advantage of such vulnerability.

Tehya's mother could not help it; her thoughts turned to their mating night, desperately hoping he would be gentle with her. As he had just said, he had gone a long time without a mate. Tehya's father squeezed his mate's hand, thinking the same thing. The male was massive, and their daughter was a waif by comparison. He did not like to think about it—to them, she was still their offspring.

The late summer sun was finally setting, drawing down the peace of twilight. Tehya's nerves were frayed, and she was exhausted from the excitement of being chosen, followed quickly by the tension of waiting for what was to happen between her and her mate.

After they finished and as the evening was ending, Khon'Tor led Tehya back to the Leader's Quarters. Some of the females had asked for permission to prepare his living space for his new mate, and he had allowed it. They had everything gathered together, and when he announced he was taking a mate, they had scurried down and decorated it as they had for Akule and the other males.

Tehya, therefore, stepped into a large living space of generous appointment with fresh flowers scenting the air. The females had placed Lavender and Rose petals in the sleeping mat, which they had overstuffed in the way the mats always were when someone took a mate.

She looked around nervously. She had heard Khon'Tor's earlier words of reassurance, but she was not reassured. She had attended the Ashwea Tare meetings, and she understood the mechanics of mating. But considering how the male standing beside her dwarfed her by comparison, she was afraid.

Khon'Tor watched her with building anticipation. Tomorrow was going to be a trying day for him, and he needed his mind as clear as possible. Release was what he needed and how much more convenient this was going to be, if not as fulfilling, than going out hunting and overpowering a female.

Tehya was so small. He would have to be very careful not to forget himself with her. This was her first mating, and he had planned to indoctrinate her slowly and carefully over time. But he might no longer have the luxury of time. Tonight, he would take it as slow as he could. Given that he could survive the hearing tomorrow with his freedom intact, he did not want another mate who despised him. If he were going to bend her to his appetites, he would first have to win her trust.

Khon'Tor brought a cold drink to Tehya and bid her sit down. She looked grateful for something to do, even if it were only to sip some water. Her eyes kept wandering to the oversized and fluffy sleeping mat. He wondered if she were thinking about how it had been a long time since his first mate died.

Khon'Tor went to Tehya, took one of her hands, and led her over to the sleeping area. He motioned for her to sit down on the inviting puffy mat, and she did, looking up at him like a captured fawn. He felt himself stir at the fright in her eyes. He would use her fear to help him complete the act with her, but he would not use it to fan his lust higher than he could control.

And then, for some reason, sitting next to this tiny, vulnerable young female looking up to him for reassurance and guidance, something shifted within Khon'Tor.

He remembered who he used to be, how he used to be, when he and Hakani were first paired. Khon'Tor had not always been as he was now. When he was first joined with Hakani, he had hopes of a successful union. He took his time with her, trying to ensure her pleasure before his. He knew that it was the male's responsibility to make the female want to come to him. For some reason, with Tehya he now felt a reconnection with that lost part of himself.

He sat down next to her and looked at her. She was truly beautiful, and so very trusting. And then Khon'Tor did something he had not done for ages and ages. He had even forgotten about it.

He leaned over and gently kissed Tehya. Then he sat back and looked at her again. Her golden-brown hair was unique. It was longer than most of the females kept theirs, and it trailed down her back, across her shoulders and down her arms. He picked up an end, curling it between his fingers. She smelled of warm spices. Somehow Khon'Tor had found his way back to a gentler part of himself, a part he had locked away when Hakani turned against him.

Khon'Tor forced himself to slow down. *Perhaps this is a bad idea. What if I cannot control myself with her?* The stress of the day and the anticipation of tomorrow were weighing heavily on him. And her soft, innocent presence nervously awaiting his next move was sucking the self-control from his marrow.

He realized that he was responding to her. Not to his desire to dominate or frighten her, but a natural longing to mate with her in its purest and simplest form. "Tehya, I want to claim you as my own. But I do not wish to hurt you."

Was he saying these things? He did not recognize himself.

"But we are paired now. I know it will hurt the first time. It has been explained to me," replied Tehya. Khon'Tor sighed; he knew her words were a vapid understatement of how painful the experience could be.

"I do not think you understand how much," he said. If only Tehya were not so small; it made it impossible not to hurt her. At that moment, he came up with a solution, how he could gain his release, yet not make it so painful for her that she would never let him touch her again.

"I want to please you," she said softly, raising her head to kiss him in return. Her kiss was soft and yielding, and it stirred his desire. *When was the last time a female ever wanted to please me*? he wondered. If seemed his relationships with them had always been waged on a battlefront.

But there was nothing in this female that made him want to hurt her. No hint of defiance. No challenge to his authority. No terror. She was innocent and humble, and he was having a different reaction to her than he had ever had with any female.

"Lie down with me. Just lie down and let me touch you and see if you can enjoy what I am doing without worrying about what is coming next. Can you try to do that?" She nodded yes and stretched out next to him.

Khon'Tor lay down, propped up by one elbow. When she closed her eyes, he began gently, first stroking her hair, tracing the side of her cheek with the back of his fingers, and then running his thumb across her soft lips—then down the side of her neck again, once again fingering the curls at the end of her hair.

She sighed at his touch.

He ran his hand down the side of her waist, along the curve of her hips. Careful not to touch her intimately, just letting her enjoy the feel of his hands on her without any demands. Down her legs, her calves, softly rolling each of her little toes, then back up, across her belly—anywhere he could give her pleasure. He took his time and let the moments stretch out as he focused simply on pleasing her.

"Khon'Tor." She said his name.

He knew he had stirred desire in her. But he knew it was also way too soon. He needed to inflame her lust for him in order to block out how much it was going to hurt when he took her.

He would have to build her to that point over time. Time—the one thing he was suddenly not sure he had. "I do not wish to hold back much longer, Tehya. But I will not let myself hurt you. Please trust me to lead you through this, to lead us through this, as gently as I can."

Khon'Tor rolled her over to him. He drew her one leg over his, her thigh resting on his hip, to where he was in contact with her.

She straightened as he pressed his desire for her between her legs. He was not going to pierce her maidenhood, but he moved against her, pressing himself slightly into her. It was all he could do not to bury himself deep inside. Instead, he took his hand and made gentle swirling motions where he knew she needed it.

She submitted to him touching her so intimately. She turned her head and moaned and moved against his hand. Knowing she wanted him inflamed him. He took his time and waited for the signs, the blossoming, expansive wave of indescribable pleasure swelling and then contracting within her. Knowing he had pleased her pushed him to the edge; entering her the shallowest bit, he took hold of himself and pressed into her just enough that he spent himself also.

She curled into a ball, enjoying the waves of pleasure still rippling through her. Khon'Tor's hands running over her body had lit desire within Tehya, first a slow glow that soon became a burning ember. They had explained the mechanics in the Ashwea Tare, but she had not believed them when they told her she would want it to happen. It was delicious and wonderful, and her fear had dissipated like leaves blowing away in the wind.

Khon'Tor wrapped himself around her. She felt safe and protected. Just before she drifted off to sleep, she took his hand and hugged it to her chest.

Khon'Tor woke in the middle of the night to quiet, muffled sounds coming from the corner of the sleeping area. He slipped off the bed and went over to Tehya who was sitting propped up in the corner, her head resting on crossed arms, crying.

He got up and went to kneel before her. He lifted

her head with his hand. "Tehya, what is wrong? Why are you crying?"

She looked up at him, but tears continued down her cheeks.

"Come back and tell me what is wrong." He led her to the mat and held her close against him. "Now, why are you crying? Are you homesick?"

"No, Adoeete. Well, yes, but no, that is not why I am crying."

She had addressed him as Adoeete, the term for Great Leader. But that was not what he wanted to be to her.

"You must not call me that. I am not Adoeete to you. You are my mate. You are my equal. You are not beneath me. Only in times of crisis should you consider me as your *Leader*. Now, why do you cry? Did I hurt you after all?" His tone was serious, but not unkind.

"No. No, you have been very considerate. That is exactly it; I was so frightened and you were so gentle with me. You are not as I feared. But there is more than that; you are a legend among the People. I do not know if I can be the mate of a legend."

"When I am with you, I am not a legend. I am just Khon'Tor. Now, promise me that I did not hurt you." Anyone overhearing this would never have believed this was Khon'Tor—at least not one they had ever known.

"I was terrified of being mated. But it was—it was

so pleasurable. I would like to do it again if you do not mind."

Khon'Tor actually chuckled. "We will. But you must trust me and do just as I say. You may not understand everything that is happening, but you must accept that it is for your good. Can you accept that?"

"Yes," answered Tehya softly.

It was so endearing; she was so gentle and unassuming. Her willing submission to Khon'Tor was stirring him as much as had his forced domination of the others. Somehow her gentle spirit had broken through his armor of anger and spite. "Well then, good. Because I have a plan," and they both laughed together at that for some reason. "Now, go back to sleep, and we will start putting *my plan* in place tomorrow night."

Khon'Tor fell asleep hoping that there would be a tomorrow night with Tehya. But he could not be sure. It would all depend on what happened at Adia's hearing the next day.

CHAPTER 8

Morning came. Khon'Tor awoke pleased that Tehya was still lying next to him. He felt uneasiness in the pit of his stomach as he remembered that today was the day of the hearing.

During the previous meeting, he had been so sure of himself. Confident he would thwart Adia's accusation as being her word against his. But now he did not feel the same. What had changed?

Tehya stirred next to him, opened her amber eyes, and smiled up at him trustingly.

That was what had changed for Khon'Tor. The previous day it had been a question of who would and who would not believe him—who would side with him and who would side with Adia. It mattered to him; the People's opinion of him was his Achilles heel, but without proof, the High Council could not strip him of his leadership, and in time, any fervor would die back down. But now there was Tehya. And he did not want Tehya to think less of him.

How could this have happened? I do not even know the female. I merely picked her from the available maidens. How is it that I can care so deeply about what she thinks of me?

Khon'Tor felt as if his armor of confidence now had a fatal flaw in it, a weak spot through which a crushing blow could be delivered. And it was located right over his heart.

Acaraho rose earlier than the others and went to check on the meeting room and line up the guards as before. Chiefs Ogima Adoeete and Is'Taqa were in the eating area when he passed through. He did not speak with them, wanting to avoid any appearance of collusion.

Acaraho was a male of great honor, which made Kurak'Kahn's words to him all the more cutting.

The rest of the morning was a blur. Before long, it was time to convene the hearing.

The High Council members sat at the long rock table as before. It was customary for the Overseer to sit in the center, but Kurak'Kahn preferred not to, as he preferred to walk around and did not like being trapped in the middle by those seated to his left and right.

Khon'Tor and the others were already assembled

by the time Adia came in. The Leader had told Tehya to spend the morning with her parents as they would be leaving today. He would find her later. He hoped that when he did, he would not be escorted by guards.

Acaraho was in his official capacity and so did not come in at the same time as his mate. Nadiwani was with Adia at her request.

If Kurak'Kahn had slept the night before, it did not affect his mood. He appeared to be angry already. Clearly, the drama that was life in the community of the People of the High Rocks was wearing on him.

He called the meeting to order. "This hearing of the High Council has been called at the request of Adia, Healer of the People of the High Rocks. Adia, step forward, and state the matter you have asked us to hear."

Adia stepped forward. She had prayed for the words to come, and she squared her shoulders and remembered who she was, daughter of the great Adoeete Apenimon'Mok, the most revered of all Leaders.

"Kurak'Kahn, Overseer of the High Council, and High Council members. Many years ago, I came before you admitting that I had broken one of the Sacred Laws of the People. I confessed to you that I was with offspring, a condition forbidden by the Second Law to a Healer or a Healer's Helper. At that time, you asked me to name the father, and I refused, stating that it had no bearing on the fact of my condition. Lesharo'Mok of the People of the Deep Valley, you stated that the father of my offspring bore equal responsibility for breaking the Second Law. You went on to ask if he were aware that he was the father, to which I answered yes. I told you that I would not give you my reason for withholding his identity but asked that you would trust that they were honorable and not meant to impede justice in any way."

She paused to collect her thoughts. "Yesterday, I came to you and told you that I had carried a second offspring—unbeknownst to me. I did not know I was carrying two until the time of the second birth. As we closed the hearing yesterday, you, Kurak'Kahn, openly accused me of using continued poor judgment, starting with allowing myself to be seeded. You went so far as to say I should consider whether I was fit to remain the Healer to the People of the High Rocks."

Even as she repeated them, the words were stinging her again. "Kurak'Kahn, Overseer of the High Council, long ago, you spoke to me of justice and mercy. You said that all of us deserve judgment, but that few of us do not deserve mercy. It was your *mercy* that forced me to give up one of my offspring, to be handed over to a female who hated me and later tried to take my child's life. Your *mercy* has given me a life of immeasurable pain and suffering. I would hate to have experienced the life that your *judgment* would have given me."

Adia could tell Kurak'Kahn was becoming

angrier by the minute, but she knew he was obliged to let her make her statement.

"You talked about Khon'Tor's great love for his people, and his sacrifice on their behalf. And the First of the First Laws which tells us that the needs of the community must come before the needs of the individual. Then, in the next breath, you spoke of your disappointment in Acaraho, High Protector of the People of the High Rocks—a male who has served the People with exemplary honor and valor. A male who has suffered alongside me in my sin, though bearing no responsibility for my condition. A male who has lived above reproach—yet who has had his character questioned and tarnished unfairly and unjustifiably throughout all these years."

She turned to look at Acaraho.

"A male who stepped up to become a father to my son, Nootau, when his real father would not."

Deafening silence. The words seemed to hang in the air. *Real father*.

She turned back to face them. "I never wanted to be standing here before you. I was willing to bear the brunt of your judgment—yes, your *judgment*—as well as the years of injustice that I have suffered. I was prepared to live under the shadow and bear the disgrace of being the fallen Healer. I was prepared to live with it forever—for the sake of the People I love. Because I *am* the Healer of the People of the High Rocks. And because I *have* put the needs of the community above my own pain.

"But," Adia shook her head and raised her hand. "No longer. It is time for the truth to be known. For years and years, I have struggled and wrestled with what the consequences may be. I pray that the Great Spirit will give you the wisdom to weigh the crimes that were committed against me and find a solution that does not destroy my people, because I was never able to find one.

"The crime of my seeding was not mine, Kurak'Kahn. And it was not Acaraho's. It was Khon'-Tor's—Leader of the People of the High Rocks."

None of the High Council members moved. The room was deathly silent.

Adia turned and looked directly at Khon'Tor before continuing. "The crime of my seeding was a crime committed against me, not by me. Struck down, attacked, barely conscious, I was taken Without My Consent and left to die. It was not I who broke the Second Law, that a Healer could never mate. It was Khon'Tor who broke the First Law, Never Without Her Consent. But because of the First of the First Laws, that the needs of the People come before the needs of any single member, I have kept the truth hidden all these years. I have kept it hidden to spare the People from a truth that will destroy the peace and trust in their leadership that is necessary for our community to survive."

More silence.

She turned back to face the High Council members. "Until yesterday, Khon'Tor did not know that he had fathered two offspring. He only knew of his son, Nootau. Kurak'Kahn, you asked Nootau to withdraw his claim on Nimida when I explained that they were brother and sister. Once I revealed that Nimida was Nootau's sister, and you ruled that his right to claim Nimida was valid, Khon'Tor withdrew his claim to be paired with her. You praised Khon'Tor for *an act of valor, which was in truth only his realization that he could not mate with his own daughter.*

"And I still would have let it go, but I cannot and will not continue to let you vilify a male like Acaraho for the crime of another who does not deserve your praise and adoration."

Moments passed. Khon'Tor sat through everything Adia said. He kept looking at the High Council members, waiting for someone to say something, but the enormity of what Adia was telling them was numbing.

To a man, every member of the High Council sat motionless, trying to process everything Adia had just told them. Their long-held beliefs about what the truth was had just been shattered, and silent pandemonium raged through each member's mind.

All these years—when they assumed that Adia and Acaraho had broken the Second Law out of human frailty—they had forced the female to give up the offspring she was carrying, assuming her guilt for her troublesome predicament. They had claimed they were showing her mercy, but in truth, had shown none.

Kurak'Kahn realized that this was what Chief Ogima Adoeete had been saying yesterday. He had been beseeching Khon'Tor to come forward and admit his crime. He had been calling for a return to honor among the leadership—but he was not speaking of Acaraho and Adia—he was speaking of Khon'Tor.

It was a tremendous blow to everything in which they believed. All these years of blaming Adia and Acaraho for a crime neither had committed. Praising Khon'Tor as he sat in silence and let them both take the blame while the Leader allowed his own son to be turned over to a female who hated them all.

Kurak'Kahn realized that the anguish Adia must have suffered was more than any of them could fathom.

Finally, he spoke, subdued. "Adia, do you have anything else you wish to add at this time?"

"No, Overseer. Not at this time. But I reserve the right to speak later if I so choose." With that, she sat down next to Nadiwani.

Ogima Adoeete was praying to the Great Spirit for truth to prevail. Is'Taqa was ready, willing to verify Adia's story at whatever moment necessary. Nadiwani was barely managing not to scream at what she had just learned. Acaraho had his eyes locked on Khon'Tor and was prepared to react should the Leader make even the slightest movement toward Adia.

Khon'Tor had led the People through all these years with an iron will. His heart beat with a warrior's rhythm. He believed in the First and Second Laws; in fact, he had been faulted for being unyielding in administering them. At his core, he cared about the People and willingly bore the burden of responsibility for their welfare. He never asked for sympathy or support, though it was true that the People's opinion of him was his weakness.

Whereas other Leaders might be more mellow, Khon'Tor was driven. Where another might be forgiving of weaknesses, Khon'Tor expected perfection. He demanded loyalty, and anything less provoked his ire. When he rose to speak, the room fell silent. He had the People's respect, and they took comfort in his strength and conviction, even if they did not always agree with his decisions.

Khon'Tor was a fighter. It was not in his nature to be otherwise. His will kept him moving forward, never questioning its wisdom or right to do so. He had never faltered in taking action. If every day of his life had to be a battle, he would never question that it should be otherwise.

Kurak'Kahn turned and addressed him. "Khon'Tor, Leader of the People of the High Rocks. A charge of breaking First Law has been brought against you. Do you wish to speak to the accusations made?"

Khon'Tor had his plan laid out in his mind. He had only to discredit Adia; to create a reasonable doubt about what she was alleging. *Why had she taken so long to come forward with this story? How outrageous was this claim! Why had the females attending her not found any evidence of this supposed violation?* He had only to point out that she was fighting for her position as Healer, reinforcing Kurak'Kahn's statement of yesterday that questioned her fitness to be Healer.

Khon'Tor had an arsenal of tactics and counter-tactics ready to break Adia's accusation free of its foundation.

And he could not bring himself to use any of them.

He tried to summon the will to fight so that it would bring him to his feet. It had always manifested unbidden. He had never before had to call it into being. Where was that unrelenting drive to win at any cost?

But something had changed. Khon'Tor did not want to fight any longer. He yearned for peace. He yearned for the war between himself and Adia to end. An unfamiliar movement was stirring within him. As Khon'Tor sat there with all eyes upon him, for the first time in his life, he was unsure of what to do.

And out of the flames of his confusion, unbeknownst to Khon'Tor, rose his chance for redemption.

Adia was feeling everything in the room. She had found peace in her decision finally to stand in the truth. And when she had made that decision, the turmoil in her dissipated. Her mind and heart quieted down. And from within the silence, her seventh sense re-engaged.

She could feel Nadiwani's abject confusion and bewilderment over what was going on. She felt her friend's self-recrimination for how she had judged Adia and Acaraho, even scolding them for their weakness in surrendering to their base desires.

She felt Acaraho's steely readiness to spring into action at the least sign of trouble, his deep love for her, and his unrelenting commitment to protect her at any cost.

Adia could feel the confusion in the High Council members' minds, swirling in an onslaught of conflicting thoughts. She realized that Kurak'Kahn was fighting for self-control, feeling the impact of her words and struggling to find sense in it as he waited for Khon'Tor to speak.

Chief Ogima Adoeete and Is'Taqa were deep in

prayer, fighting on the spiritual planes. They were standing in their belief that truth and honor, in the end, would prevail.

She knew that they both believed her, had perhaps known for some time that Khon'Tor was the father and not Acaraho. But how? In Chief Ogima, it seemed to live as a fact of reasoning, a deduction drawn from observation, and the wisdom that comes from experience. But in Is'Taqa, it was something more. It was a knowing; it registered as a fact in his mind. Almost as if he knew for certain— Then she felt Is'Taqa's mind reaching out to her, inviting her in.

Suddenly Adia was standing in the cold, hiding behind snow-covered bushes, watching a drama unfold which her mind could not accept. It was dim, a dark shadowed scene. She could not tell who they were, but she watched as two figures met on a narrow path; as after a brief exchange the larger figure struck the smaller, knocking him to the ground. Then she saw another blow delivered as the smaller tried to rise. Her blood ran cold as the larger one assumed an unmistakable position over the other, and her mind fought the reality of the abomination which was taking place. After he had finished, the perpetrator stood for a while in thought. Then, seeming to search in the snow, and finding what he was looking for, bent down over the female he had just violated and placed something in her hand. Finally satisfied, he turned to leave, and she ducked back under cover as the larger figure passed by. It was Khon'Tor, the Leader of the

People of the High Rocks. She was waiting. Waiting for him to get far enough away. Then she was finally running to the fallen figure on the snow—

Adia released the vision Is'Taqa had opened up to her mind; she looked over at Is'Taqa and he at her. The Second Chief nodded very slightly. He knew she understood that he had seen the entire attack.

How Adia wished she had known before. All the anguish she had endured over whether to reveal what Khon'Tor had done—had she known that Is'Taqa witnessed it all, they could have shared the struggle together. Both had suffered in silence; she not wanting to risk the destruction of her people, and he not wanting to risk the generations of peace between their two tribes.

Adia's hand went to her heart in a gesture of thanks and understanding to Is'Taqa. They had borne their burdens well.

And from Khon'Tor, she felt an emptiness. No, a stillness. This was not the male she had known and fought with all these years. Where was the raging anger, the sense of insult, the boisterous denial of any wrongdoing on his part, ever? Where was the warrior coiling within him, ready to stand up and come at her throwing everything he had?

Adia had arrived braced for a counterattack, ready to bear the onslaught of accusations and aspersions cast upon her character—picking up where Kurak'Kahn had left off yesterday in questioning her right to remain Healer.

She had prepared herself for anything and everything, with no holds barred—whatever it took to discredit her and ridicule her claim of his attack. He was Khon'Tor, Leader of the People of the High Rocks. He was a warrior, and surrender was not in his blood.

Or was he? Where was this male who had battled and resented her for years, the reason for which she had never known until Hakani revealed that Adia had been his First Choice? For years she had paid for an offense to his pride that she had never levied. She had never rejected him, yet in his mind and heart, somehow by being removed from the pairing options she had spurned him, and she had paid for that imaginary affront at every turn.

But Adia could sense none of this within Khon'-Tor. Here was someone she did not recognize. Was it a trick? If so, how could it be? Khon'Tor was clever, but not even he could fake this total dissolution of his former self.

The People say that when truth is spoken, the speaker stands in the presence of the Great Spirit. It may be an unflattering truth. It may be a painful truth. It may be a truth that brings consequences one would rather avoid. But there is power in the truth that sets the winds of salvation in motion.

Finally, Khon'Tor stood.

He looked over at Adia. And for the first time, he saw her. Not the foe he had been battling all these years. Not the female who had spurned his love and deserved his hate in return. Not an adversary to be vanquished but a female he had fabricated into an enemy and then waged war against. A female who had no understanding of what she had done to deserve his anger, nor why they were even locked in battle. Then, with the worst of all his sins—his punishment for the imaginary crimes he had assigned to her—he had wronged her in a way for which there could be no restitution.

A low growl came up from Acaraho's throat as Khon'Tor continued to look at Adia. "Move along. Get on with it," the High Protector said under his breath.

Khon'Tor turned toward Acaraho, raised his hand in what appeared to be a gesture of peace, and quietly said, "There is no need, Acaraho. There is no need for any more of this. It is time for this war to end. It will end today, and I will be the one to end it.

"Adia, Healer of the People of the High Rocks, has accused me of assaulting her. She stated that I attacked her, and then, while she was lying helpless in a state of unconsciousness, I mated her Without Her Consent, breaking the Tenth of the First Laws. Afterward, I callously left her to die, alone in the cold, to cover up my crimes against her."

Khon'Tor took a few steps closer to the High Council table, Acaraho still watching his every move.

"It is also the Healer's assertion that I have stood silently while she suffered the judgment and condemnation of our community and the High Council for breaking Second Law by willingly mating, and by that act being seeded. When in truth, she committed no crime. It was my crime against her that put her in violation of her vows as a Healer. Lastly, through my own cowardice, I allowed Acaraho, High Protector of the People of the High Rocks, to take the blame for seeding her offspring—which we now know to be not one offspring but two, a son and a daughter—and letting his reputation be tarnished for a crime I committed."

Khon'Tor turned to Adia and asked her, "Adia Adoeete, is that a fair summation of your charges against me?"

Adia answered, "It is accurate, yes."

Khon'Tor turned away from her to face the High Council again, now directly in front of Kurak'Kahn, the Overseer. "Let the record show then, that my response to the accusations against me by Adia, Healer of the People of the High Rocks, is that every one of them is true. I stand guilty as accused."

Every Leader was taught that there is a time to yield the blade and a time to lay the blade down. And that wisdom resides in knowing when to do which. Up until moments before, these had only been poetic words, a soothing tale perhaps to comfort those weaker-willed Leaders who did not have the courage to fight for what they believed in.

But now, for the first time in his life, Khon'Tor finally understood the meaning.

"There is a time to yield the blade, and there is a time to lay down the blade. Wisdom resides in knowing when to do which."

Khon'Tor had just laid down his blade of lies and deception.

Nadiwani almost came out of her chair. Acaraho was momentarily stunned but recovered quickly for fear this was another trick. But it could not be. Khon'Tor had just admitted his guilt without reservation.

Adia, too, could not believe what she had just heard. She had been prepared for Khon'Tor's attacks, his denials, his repudiation of her claims. She was not prepared for him to admit to everything. But Khon'Tor had said it was time for the war to end. And that he would be the one to end it.

The High Council members could barely contain themselves. All these years of blaming Adia and Acaraho. Maybe not openly blaming them, but in truth, in each of their hearts, they had faulted the couple. And now here came Khon'Tor, admitting to the most heinous of crimes, that of taking a female Without Her Consent. And not just a female—a Healer and a maiden.

Kurak'Kahn could not take it in. He had heard it, but his mind could not process it. He needed to hear it again, to have another slap in the face for it to solidify into reality. He could not leave any chance of misunderstanding.

Therefore, he asked, "Khon'Tor, please recount clearly the events of your crimes against Adia."

"As you wish. It was the beginning of the cold weather. One of the watchers had reported a Waschini riding party coming through the end of our territory. I called a general assembly and ordered everyone gathered in from outside, and I stated unequivocally that no one was to leave. I then retired to my quarters where my mate and I had a —disagreement."

"Explain what you mean by disagreement," said Kurak'Kahn.

Khon'Tor decided that if he were going to tell the truth, he might as well get it all out.

"Over the years, my relationship with Hakani became—adversarial. She had denied me for many, many years, refusing me release and refusing to bear me the offspring I need as heir to my line. I was exhausted that night and wanted only to sleep. I was awoken by her indicating to me her willingness to mate. Despite our difficult relationship, and after years of denial, I accepted her offer. Only to be told *no* at the last possible moment.

"I threatened to set her aside, to request Bak-tah Awhidi, and take another mate who would provide me with an offspring. She laughed and said that it would be impossible to have her set aside when it would soon be apparent that she was with offspring —by another man, but which offspring everyone would assume was mine. I will admit I was enraged. I most likely would have harmed her seriously had the watcher, Akule, not come to my quarters in an agitated state to tell me that the Healer had left Kthama.

"I left in search of Adia. Akule told me where he had seen her, and I found her on a narrow path. She appeared to be confused and uncertain about where she was. I offer no excuse for what I did, only a statement that I was in such an enraged state from my earlier fight with Hakani, that Adia's defiance in leaving Kthama, all the years of animosity between us and the underlying battles, somehow everything combined. And in my rage, I struck Adia for defying me. When she rose again, she steadied herself against me, and at her touch my last bit of reality slipped away and she and Hakani became one in my mind. My anger at Hakani became my anger at Adia. Then, when Adia was lying helpless on the ground, my rage turned to something else. It was then that I violated her. Knowing she was a maiden, knowing she was the Healer, I took her Without Her Consent.

"I left her to die after arranging the scene to look as if she had simply fallen and struck her head on a rock."

The Overseer's mind finally came around and accepted it. It was true. It was all true. He willed himself to be elsewhere, but to no avail, so he continued, "Khon'Tor, by the testimony of Adia Healer of the People of the High Rocks, and by your own admission of guilt, the High Council finds you guilty of the violation of the Sacred Law, Never Without Consent. This hearing is adjourned. We will reconvene tomorrow morning with our ruling regarding the punishment for your crime.

"Council members, after a short break, please return so we can discuss the testimony we have just heard," directed Kurak'Kahn.

With that, it was over—at least for the day. With the official session now ended, no one knew what to do. There were no congratulations to be made and there were no insights to be shared. It was a dark day for all the People, and none of those present, including Adia, took any pleasure in what had just happened.

"Kurak'Kahn," Khon'Tor interrupted the Overseer. "Where would you like me to go until the hearing tomorrow? Am I to be restrained?"

Khon'Tor wanted to go back to his quarters but

did not want guards showing up a while later in front of Tehya because someone had forgotten the small detail of what to do with him.

"Retire to your quarters, Khon'Tor. For the sake of protocol, Acaraho, place a guard at the end of the Leader's corridor. I do not expect any trouble, but I would be remiss if I did not put proper precautions in place." Acaraho nodded to Kurak'Kahn and went to open the stone door so they could all file out.

Everyone was lost in thought and reflection. It was too much to bear. This terrible secret—through all these years.

Chief Ogima Adoeete looked over at Khon'Tor before he left. Khon'Tor thought he saw a glimmer of compassion in the old man's eyes. But it was probably just wishful thinking.

CHAPTER 9

Whatever had happened, Khon'Tor was a changed person. He had not achieved total salvation, but he was well on his way toward it. A burden had been lifted that he had not known he was carrying. At least now the worrying, the constant looking over his shoulder, half expecting Adia to turn him in, or any number of other ways in which it could all have come crashing down upon him were gone.

The waiting was over. He had brought it all down on his own head, but there was a peace to it, nonetheless.

Khon'Tor thought of Tehya, waiting hopefully for him in his quarters. Their quarters. He had thought last night would be the only night he would have with her. Now he had been granted another. He could not bear the thought of her hearing what he had done to Adia. He wished he could go back and undo it all.

Tomorrow, everything would collapse around him, but for now, he had one last night of the wide-eyed acceptance and admiration he saw in her eyes.

Khon'Tor looked around the door to find Tehya there. She was fussing over something on the eating area worktable.

She looked up with a happy expression on her face. "Khon'Tor! I am so glad you are back. Look, I made a meal for us. We can stay here; we do not have to go to the general eating area!"

She was so pleased with herself; he could not help but smile as he went over to see what she had put together. He nodded his approval, and she lit up further.

What has this trusting soul done to me? She has healed me in some way by her innocence—by her belief in me. She has helped me find my way back to the male I was meant to be. How I wish I had a lifetime ahead with her instead of just this one night.

Tehya could see that something was wrong. "What is it, Khon'Tor? Why are you so sad? Are you not happy to see me? Have you tired of me already?" But she was joking now.

"Oh, no. Not by any means, my little mate. Not by any means at all." And Khon'Tor did as he had seen Acaraho do with Adia and picked her up and swept her off her feet. As light as a feather, he carried her over to the sleeping mat.

"Oh my! And we have not even had our evening meal yet," she laughed.

"It will keep. But I have been away too long, and we have lost time that we need to make up," kidded Khon'Tor.

As he lay her down, she leaned back up for a kiss. And all the troubles of the day melted away, and he had only one thought, and that was of being with her and pleasing her. *How do you squeeze a lifetime into one last evening*? he asked himself.

If this was to be their one night together, he wanted to be as one with her. But he did not want her last memory of them to be one of pain. He knew he had to bring her to a state of passion so great that the pleasure of release would overshadow the pain when he took her. And perhaps he could leave her some part of himself to remember him by.

"Do you recall what I told you about trusting me? Trusting that what I am doing will be only for your benefit and your pleasure?"

She nodded yes, running her fingers through the silver crest of his hair.

"You're not listening, Tehya," he scolded her.

She laughed at him, and her eyes twinkled with what he hoped were the first sparks of love.

"Yes, I am. I am to do everything you tell me to do —always? Is that correct?"

She is an imp; I am paired with an imp, he smiled to himself. "Well, then you have been paying attention. Yes, that is exactly right. We will start now. Close your eyes. Lie back again, and do not worry about what I am doing or what I might be going to do—just relax and enjoy it." He was speaking softly and kindly to her. So very unlike the distant tone that had later become so harsh and cruel when he spoke to Hakani.

Tehya laid back as told and waited. *Will it be the same as last night? Will he mate with me properly tonight? What will it be like when he does?*

Her mind was a whirlwind of questions and imaginings—until he kissed her. And then everything faded away except the two of them.

As he had the night before, he touched her oh so lightly. The slightest pressure, the softest of contact. Just enough but not enough until her body was rising to meet his hands and his lips and the warmth of him. He took his time, stirring her desire for him. Touching her but never giving her quite enough of what she wanted, teasing her to the brink of release and then stopping before she could breach the crest.

"Wait. Why did you stop? Wha—?"

"Sssh. Remember our agreement. Trust me. Now lie back again and relax. Each time you interrupt me, I have to start all over again," Khon'Tor chided her playfully.

Then his hands were on her once more, and again, he brought her to the edge of delight and then just as she was almost there, stopped his ministrations.

Tehya was screaming in her head. She opened her eyes and stared at him. Then she teased, "Are you sure you know what you are doing?"

"Hush," he chuckled. He smiled and slowly rolled her over onto him as he had done the night before, one leg over his thigh, and picked up where he had left off. Only then did he press his lust for her up against her private place, ready to enter her at just the exact moment.

When she felt him there, Tehya knew exactly what she wanted. An inner emptiness she had not known existed was aching to be filled.

His hand on her was all velvet swirls and delicious circles. Then he stopped again, only this time taking her hand and placing it where his had been.

"What?" She was not sure what he wanted, and then again, she was also afraid that maybe she did know.

"Do as I have been doing. Do not tell me you have never pleased yourself, Tehya?"

"No, I have not. I did not know we were allowed!"

He laughed and put her hand back where he wanted it and waited for her to do as he had told her.

She was a fast learner, and before too long, she had approached the threshold and was at the crest. As she was about to go over and at the first ripples of pleasure started, he shifted her under him and then with one hard thrust, forced himself through her maidenhead. Pain and ecstasy merged, and she lost track of where and who and how and everything but that moment and the emptiness that was now filled and they who were two but were now one.

As the waves of her splendor surrounded him, he delivered one more stroke, and then another, not daring to enter her fully as they spent together in simultaneous release.

After a few moments, he withdrew himself from her and lay back. She scooted over and tossed herself on top of him, enjoying the warm feel of the hard muscles of his chest and his breath rising and falling.

All the tension was gone from everywhere in his body, and Khon'Tor quietly soaked up the feeling of satisfaction. He thought about Tehya lying on him— she was a feather. A sprite. How he had not split her open, he did not know except that she had been so very ready for him. His plan had worked; he had brought her to a state of desire through building up and denying her repeatedly, so the pain of his taking her was lost in the exquisite waves of pleasure when she finally reached release.

He laid an arm across her, enjoying how wonderfully drained he felt. He had wanted to take longer, but he knew he had already hurt her, so he had allowed himself to finish quickly.

He wondered how he could have come to find such a prize as she, and how one person could turn everything around. He wondered what he had done to deserve this creature. And then it hit him. This was not a reward.

This was his punishment.

Finally, he had found happiness. Only it had come too late. He had wasted his life on anger and revenge and spite. And now, when the chance had arrived to know love, perhaps to raise his own offspring—to truly be Khon'Tor the greatest Leader of the People, with a loving mate by his side—it was all going to be ripped from his grasp as retribution for his crimes.

Somehow, the male who had committed those crimes was gone. So where was justice? The monster who had committed those crimes would not be the one to pay for them. The male here now was one who would never have committed such travesties, yet it was his debt to pay.

It was not long before she fell asleep. He pulled a coverlet over her as she lay on his chest.

Khon'Tor glanced over at his Leader's staff, propped in the corner in its usual spot. He remembered his father explaining how one day in the future, Khon'Tor would inherit the staff, and he would become the Leader of the High Rocks. And that someday, even farther into the future, Khon'Tor would turn it over to his son. But now, if he were found guilty, his staff would be broken and burned.

And the 'Tor line would end with him, in shame and disgrace.

Emotions he did not know he could feel moved through him. Regret, self-recrimination, sadness, humility. And then he did something he had not done in the longest time—he prayed to the Great Spirit.

Khon'Tor asked for forgiveness. He asked for healing for Adia, and for the others he had brutally assaulted. He thanked the Great Spirit for this female lying with him—that he had at least known love and tenderness before everything was taken away from him. And then, though he knew he did not deserve it, he asked for a way out. He prayed that a way might be made where there was none. He prayed for what he knew that he of all people did not deserve—mercy and forgiveness instead of judgment.

Depleted, he surrendered finally and let sleep take him away too, and as he did so, relinquished his hold on his last night as Adik'Tar Khon'Tor Adoeete. The one to whom others had looked for protection, leadership, and inspiration. Tomorrow he would be Khon'Tor the Fallen. The Leader who had deceived his people, and the only living male ever to have broken the Sacred Law: Never Without Her Consent.

CHAPTER 10

While Khon'Tor had gone back to his quarters, Adia and Acaraho had other matters to deal with. They were as exhausted as all the others, and they had not even had time to talk about what had just happened. Because time was running out, if they did not do something quickly, Nimida would be returning to her community with her mother's sister.

Nadiwani had left with them, her mind still reeling from learning that Nootau was Khon'Tor's son. Nootau was the rightful heir to Khon'Tor's leadership. Nootau had said he would never want to be Leader, but she did not know if that was just the careless musings of a young mind, or if he knew himself well enough to know that this was true. There was too much to figure out, and it was all such a disaster. Nadiwani could not deal with her guilt over all these years of thinking Adia and Acaraho were weak. She was too ashamed even to talk to them about it.

When Adia stopped to talk to her before they went into the Great Chamber, Nadiwani could not look her in the eyes.

"Nadiwani, please; please. We can talk about it later, but now we need to find Nimida and figure out how we are going to prevent her from returning to the People of the Great Pines."

Nadiwani tried to shake off her guilt and help Adia with this problem. She had the rest of her life to apologize for what she had thought and the things she had said. Instead, she offered, "When I was talking with Nimida, she told me she has no close family. She has only the female, her aunt, who came with her. I do not know what happened to her other family. Perhaps we could speak with the aunt and see if there is a way that Nimida could stay with us."

Adia wondered if she should tell Nimida that she was her mother. But she did not know what the young female knew about her history. "We need to talk to her to find out what she knows about her past and start there."

And Adia and Nadiwani set out to find Nimida of the Great Pines. But Nimida was nowhere to be found.

Finally, they checked her community's temporary living quarters and found her there, alone. She stood up as they apologized for intruding and introduced themselves.

"Yes, I remember you. You are Nadiwani, the Healer's Helper. And you are Adia the Healer; we have not met, but I know who you are. You and your mate were the first couple paired." Nimida was gracious and soft-spoken. Adia could not stop looking at her. It was all she could do not to hug her.

"I want to talk to you, Nimida. It is my son Nootau who was supposed to be paired with you. I want to make sure that you know his change of mind was no reflection on you."

"Nadiwani already talked to me about that, Adik'-Tar. I understand, I do. I am disappointed; I must be honest. I was looking forward to having a family of my own."

With that, an opening appeared, and Adia stepped through it. "Do you not have any family back home?"

"I have only Kinta, my mother's sister. There is no one else. I came here expecting never to go back, but now, I must." Her voice dropped at the end.

Nadiwani asked her to sit down with them, "Do you not want to go back, Nimida? Is something wrong there?"

"No. Well, no. But I am ready to move on with my life. Kinta and I came here prepared for me to be paired, and now, if I go back, I will not know what to do with myself." She was so open and honest, and it touched their hearts.

Nadiwani took the lead. "Would you like to stay here with us, Nimida? If you do not want to go back, we would be glad to have you here. We are a large community. Our land is rich in resources, and there are many here who would be glad to help you find your place. Do you have a calling?"

"If I have a calling, I have not been able to work out what it is. What do you mean, stay here with you? Is Nootau changing his mind—or is he likely to?"

"Nadiwani means that we would take you into our family. We would find you living quarters near ours, introduce you to the other females who would teach you whatever new skills you want to learn. You would be one of the People of the High Rocks. It would not be what you were expecting exactly, but it would be a change. And you would not have to go back to the Great Pines." Adia spoke gently, trying not to push.

"As far as Nootau is concerned, no. But there will be more pairings. And there are many other fine unpaired males to meet. You may find who you are looking for without the High Council making the match. And then, if you decide to pair, you can petition them at the next ceremony."

Nimida thought about it a moment. It was true, not every pair was selected by the High Council. It was not unheard of for a relationship to develop and be sanctioned later by the High Council. It was not what she had expected, but at least it was a way out.

"When would I have to decide?" She wanted to stay, but she needed to talk to Kinta too—not that her aunt would care, but as a courtesy. Perhaps this was better; she would not be paired, but there was still time for that.

Adia spoke first. "I do not know when your people are traveling back, but at least by then. If you choose to go back, you will have to leave with them because it is too far to travel by yourself. If you decide to stay, ask any of the guards to come and find one of us. In the meantime, we will make arrangements for you in case you do decide to stay."

And then Adia laid her hand on top of the young female's and added, "And we hope you do, both Nadiwani and I."

Just then, Kinta returned to the quarters. The two visitors stood up to greet her. Kinta gave them a curt hello but then turned to Nimida and asked why she had not yet packed everything and what the hold-up was.

That explained a lot to both Adia and Nadiwani. Whatever relationship there was between Nimida and Kinta, it was not a warm or welcoming one. Now they hoped even more fervently that the young female would stay.

They left and went to find Mapiya, who had helped Acaraho with much of the preparation. She might know where Nimida could stay for a few days until all the guests had left and while everyone reshuffled back to their quarters. If nothing else, they knew that Mapiya would let Nimida stay with her for a while.

For Nimida, it was not a difficult decision. She just had to let Kinta know. Seeing no point in delaying, Nimida started separating her belongings from Kinta's, putting them into a separate pile. "Kinta. I am separating our things. I am not going back with you to the Great Pines. I am going to stay here at the High Rocks."

Kinta looked over at Nimida with no reaction. Then she shrugged her shoulders, "Well, we were not planning for you to return anyway, so do whatever you want." She paused. "I hope you can find some peace here, Nimida," Kinta continued. "I know you have been unhappy since your mother died."

"Thank you, Kinta," said Nimida, surprised by her aunt's unusual expression of compassion. "Then it is settled, and I will tell them I am staying. I am so glad I have my Keeping Stones." Her Keeping Stones were all the personal items she had, other than her wraps and the supplies they had brought for the long trip.

She addressed her aunt again. "I am going to find the Healer and let her know. I have now separated your things from mine. If I do not see you again, Kinta, since I do not know when you are all leaving, thank you for bringing me here."

It was the only thing she could think to thank her for. She knew that Kinta would be relieved to be rid of her. *So that is it. No warm goodbye. I doubt Kinta will even give me a final hug. It is just as if we were deciding what cutting tool to use, not an entire change of direction for my life.* Nimida sighed. *At least it is a change. It cannot be as lonely as going back to the Great Pines.*

She practically skipped down the corridor to find the first guard she could and ask him where to find the Healer and her Helper.

The guard did not know, of course, but suggested she look in the large assembly areas. He also suggested that she let Acaraho know she was looking for them if he came by.

☾

Nimida found them soon enough; they were already talking to Mapiya. As the young female approached, Nadiwani reached out to her and motioned her into the circle.

"Mapiya, this is Nimida, the female we were talking about. Nimida, Mapiya says you are welcome to stay with her for as long as necessary, until we can make other arrangements. Have you come to tell us you are staying?" Nadiwani asked.

Adia was holding her breath.

"Yes, I am. I just told Kinta. I do not have many things, only my wraps and my Keeping Stones."

Nadiwani and Adia forced themselves not to look

at each other. Between the Keeping Stones and the marks Nadiwani had made on the twins, there was no doubt of her identity. But Adia did not need any of that; she knew this was her daughter.

Kthama was starting to empty as more and more of their guests left for home. There were days of work remaining to return everything to normal. The High Council members were still present because there was still the second meeting they intended to hold about the future of the People, and they had to complete their ruling on Khon'Tor's crimes.

By the end of the day, Nimida was settled in with Mapiya. Once again, Acaraho and Adia had too much on their minds to enjoy the fact that they were paired. They had still not joined together in real-time, though there was great joy in being able to show affection openly toward each other. So, as Tehya and Khon'Tor were sleeping soundly together, Acaraho and Adia found their rest. It was good they were so exhausted; otherwise neither of them would have slept with the stress of tomorrow hanging over their heads.

Morning came too soon. Adia woke first, greeted by a twisting in her stomach. Today was the day of the High Council ruling against Khon'Tor. Try as she could all the years during which she had struggled with it, Adia could never imagine what punishment the High Council would decide if it ever came to this. She steeled herself for what was to come next. In her heart, she felt it was one of the saddest days ever in the history of the People. Next to her father, Apenimon'Mok, she had believed there was no greater Leader than Khon'Tor. All the People would suffer this loss, not just those in her community.

And it had finally arrived; today was the day she would find out just how deep their wisdom reached. Justice was about to be delivered.

Khon'Tor took his leave of Tehya, asking her if she would like him to arrange for some of the other females to look after her—perhaps show her around so she could start getting used to Kthama.

Tehya thanked him but said she was happy in their quarters for now.

How different she is from Hakani, who could not wait to parade the fact that she was the Leader's mate.

He looked around his quarters before leaving. He made a note that they would need to do something about the huge stone door, as Tehya would never be able to move it on her own. He again left it ajar for her, knowing that the guard was stationed at the end of the corridor.

There was no threat to Tehya, but, regardless, it did give him comfort to know that one of Acaraho's males had been placed there, even though it was to keep watch on him, not to protect her.

On his way out, he stopped to talk to the guard. "She is free to come and go as she wishes. Please stay and see to it if she has any needs."

Then Khon'Tor took the longest walk of his life, leaving behind Tehya and a future he had never dreamed possible.

He was one of the first to arrive, but before long all the others had shown up. He could not name the feeling that hung in the air. A combination of tension and solemnity, it carried an air of endings.

Kurak'Kahn motioned for everyone still standing to be seated, and he opened the hearing with a face of stone.

"The High Council is reconvened in the matter of the crimes committed by Khon'Tor, Leader of the People of the High Rocks, against the Healer, Adia Adoeete."

Had there ever in the history of the People been such a travesty? Next to Adoeete Apenimon'Mok, Kurak'Kahn, like Adia, had believed that there was no greater Leader than Khon'Tor. It was a sad day for all the People, not just those of Khon'Tor's community.

"The High Council has come to a determination

in this matter. Khon'Tor, Leader of the People of the High Rocks, stand before us."

Khon'Tor got up and stood before the Overseer and the other High Council members. Whatever they had decided, he was resigned to accepting it.

"Khon'Tor," continued the Overseer. "Having heard the statement of Adia the Healer of the People of the High Rocks and the statement you made, there is no doubt as to your guilt in this matter. You violated First Law, taking the Healer Without Her Consent. Only once before in the memory of our people has this law been broken. Based on the nature of it, it goes against all our beliefs about the sovereignty of our females, and their revered position among our people. In this case, the severity of the crime is magnified by the fact that the female you violated was not only a maiden but *the Healer of your own people*.

"We have heard and considered your story about the events leading up to the crimes you committed. Without excusing it, we can understand that this was a single act, a crime resulting from a storm of factors, perhaps building over years and coming together with tragic results.

"However, beyond whatever mitigating forces might have softened the punishment you deserve for those acts alone, the fact remains that you allowed the Healer to suffer humiliation and condemnation for year after year following your violation of her. Whereas you might have been shown the slightest amount of mercy in this singular regard, there is no defense possible for your calculated, cold-hearted treatment of her thereafter."

From Kurak'Kahn's opening remarks, Khon'Tor knew their punishment of him was going to be severe. He wondered how much their guilt in the matter was to be eased by the harshness of his penalty.

"At any time during these passing years, you could have admitted your crime. You could have come to us and asked for mercy and understanding. You could have gone to Adia and done the same —*should* have done the same. You have heartlessly allowed two innocent people—the Healer, Adia, and her mate, High Protector Acaraho—to suffer for your crimes. The fact that you are in the highest position of authority makes this situation more tragic and unforgivable. And so, for these reasons, I cannot find it in my heart to show you mercy in this matter, either.

"The crimes you committed against Adia, the Healer of the High Rocks—your assault against her, your violation of her, and your continued deception in this matter, especially by a person in your position as Leader—are even more inexcusable. Few cases warrant the severest punishment the High Council can deliver. I will give you the floor now, Khon'Tor, to make your case as to why I should not order your banishment."

Banishment. The word hung in the air like a death knell.

Khon'Tor could not think of a single thing to say.

Two days ago, the old Khon'Tor would have gone on a verbal rampage, eloquently defending his actions by deflecting the blame onto a host of outside factors.

What he had done to Adia that one night had contributing factors building up to it, but they were right about the years and years of pain and suffering he had allowed them to experience by his refusal to take responsibility for his crime. Khon'Tor refused to pick up the blade he had laid down, and instead prayed that he might find peace and salvation in surrender.

And then he thought of Tehya, the sweet young female he had taken as his mate, waiting for him back in his quarters. How was this going to affect her?

"Overseer. I have nothing to say in my defense. But what of Tehya, Kurak'Kahn? What will become of her?"

It was the first time they remembered Khon'Tor ever thinking of someone other than himself.

Adia and Acaraho looked at each other from

across the room, Adia seated and Acaraho standing at his usual post. Adia knew her mate well enough to know that, as much as they were both angry with Khon'Tor, Acaraho joined her in thinking that this was merciless. *Khon'Tor would have been better off if Adia had let Acaraho kill him long ago.*

Banishment was the worst penalty that could be delivered. It was as close to a death sentence as possible; a single Sasquatch living in isolation was condemned to a life of struggle and hardship. The People were communal by nature. They depended on each other. Their social nature thrived in a setting such as their communities provided.

Even worse, for someone like Khon'Tor, to be cut off from the People and live a life of solitude would destroy him. And even if they did not mean total banishment and he would be allowed to join with another community, who would have him, knowing the nature of his crime?

Adia had reserved the right to speak. She rose and faced the High Council and picked up her blade, just as Khon'Tor had laid his down the day before.

"Kurak'Kahn; High Council. I invoke my right to speak."

"Say what you will, Healer, you have reserved that right."

But Kurak'Kahn looked impatient. There was no more severe punishment that could be delivered.

"Years ago, I stood before you as Khon'Tor does now, waiting to hear a verdict against which there is no appeal. Yours is the highest authority we have. We place our trust in you and rely on you to weigh the matters of a case and deliver a just and fair decision. But I received neither a just nor a fair decision, only judgment disguised as mercy. And having had to bear up under that sentence without recourse, I cannot stand by and let another person suffer the same fate."

Kurak'Kahn frowned.

"Of anyone, I am the last to defend what Khon'Tor did to me. And I have no defense for the years of silence on his part either. Both Acaraho and I have, as you said, suffered because of his refusal to accept responsibility for what he did. I have a son who will never know who truly fathered him because I cannot bear to have him carry the burden that he exists not as the result of an act of love but as the result of an act of brutality. And I have a daughter who does not even know who she is, because I sent her away for her protection—not just from Khon'Tor, but *also from you*. And my son will never claim his right to the leadership of the People, for the same reason that he cannot know his true parentage."

She took a step toward Khon'Tor. "I will say it again; I never intended to reveal Khon'Tor's crimes because of the damage I knew it would do to our community. It was only your disparagement of Acaraho, Kurak'Kahn, your unjust derogation of my character, and your blind willingness to praise the least innocent of us all, that finally broke my silence. Something about truth cannot bear the dark. It demands to be seen; it longs to be brought into the light of day. But had I known that this was what it would come to, I would have found a way to keep it buried forever.

"You are the High Council. You are supposed to embody the highest level of wisdom and fairness. Every time you hand down a decision, you yourselves are on trial. All the years I struggled with what he did to me, I never could come up with fair retribution. Nothing was going to undo what he did. Nothing could make it right. Nothing can take back my heartache over the fact that, since my father, the Leader I looked up to and trusted the most, betrayed me—not only in the worst way possible for a female but also in a moment of utter vulnerability. Yes, we had our difficulties, even outright battles, but when he violated me, he took more than my maidenhood, he took the Leader of my people from me."

Then she turned and looked at Khon'Tor as she said, "And without a Leader, the People perish."

Then, turning back to Kurak'Kahn. "Now you in your highest wisdom deliver a punishment that will do more damage than any I could have caused had I lodged my accusation in the beginning? All the years of suffering, both mine and Acaraho's, trying to protect our community, will have been for nothing."

As she spoke, Is'Taqa repeated softly his words of long ago, "The people can follow a corrupt Leader, as long as they do not know he is corrupt."

"My father was a Leader among Leaders. You all

know that. When he died, I thought I would also die. It was not just the loss of him as my father that I grieved, but also the loss of the knowledge that there was someone there to guide us, to look over us all. Like it or not, admit it or not, we *need* someone to look up to. Someone whom we believe has the foresight, fortitude, and determination to bring us through the dark times. Khon'Tor has been that to the People of the High Rocks for decades. And now you would rip that foundation from us, and then what? Go back to your communities and leave us somehow to claw our way out of the devastation you would bury us under? Creating impossible hardship by taking away the very thing we need *to get through the impossible hardship you yourselves would create*?

"This is not justice—it is *insanity*."

Kurak'Kahn started to rise. Chief Ogima Adoeete placed a hand on his shoulder and pushed the Overseer back down.

"Could the People follow someone else? Is there no other who could not step in and take the lead? Yes. And he is in this very room. High Protector Acaraho could take over the leadership of the People. And they would follow him gladly and with great confidence. But that is not an option. Because of the laws, leadership can only come through the Leader's bloodline. And there is no one from Khon'Tor's line except the son who can never claim his heritage. You would leave us with no leadership and in the same stroke, invoke a time of civil unrest and upheaval that you created through your collective *wisdom*?"

She took another step closer to Khon'Tor, standing within an arm's breadth of him.

"And what of Khon'Tor himself? You know that he could not survive alone. And would you send his young mate with him, an innocent female, to share in his punishment? There is no wisdom in your decision. There is no mercy, as you admitted. But there is no justice either. There is only blind retribution with no thought to the consequences.

"And if we cannot come to you for better than that, *of what good are you to us?* "

Adia's onslaught was almost complete. She had only one more blow to land. She was surprised they had stood for it but was beyond caring. No matter what Khon'Tor had done, their punishment of him was cruel and heartless, and she could not stand by and let it be delivered.

She turned to face Kurak'Kahn directly, shoulders back and standing tall. Looking him square in the eyes, she delivered the felling stroke. "I, Adia, Healer of the People of the High Rocks, *withdraw my accusation.*"

Having wielded it to its purpose, Adia put down the blade of truth.

Khon'Tor could not move. He could hardly get his mind around what had just happened. Adia had withdrawn her accusation. And once withdrawn, an accusation could not be brought forth again for rehearing.

The very female he had brutalized, demonized, disparaged, and bullied all these years had just set him free. It was without precedent for a crime of similar severity to be set aside by the accuser. But she was within her rights.

The room was dead silent.

Kurak'Kahn clenched his teeth. He wanted to object, but he had no grounds. He was powerless. She had taken the power out of his hands much as one might take a toy away from an offspring too young to be entrusted with it.

The Accuser had the right to withdraw her claim. She had spoken out before the High Council had decided the outcome and officially administered the sentence. And she had reserved the right to speak again. There was no provision for them to overrule what she had just done. She was within her rights.

Kurak'Kahn had no choice. "In the matter brought to the High Council by Adia, Healer of the People of the High Rocks against Khon'Tor, Leader of the People of the High Rocks, the accuser has withdrawn her petition. All charges against

Khon'Tor are rescinded and may not be brought again. You are free to go, Khon'Tor."

It was over.

The room was silent for some time as everyone tried to catch up with what had just happened. Kurak'Kahn was still angry. He wanted to be big enough to say something additional to Adia, something appropriate, but he could not bring himself to do it. Instead, he said to those High Council members still in the room, which included Khon'Tor, "We will reconvene after the evening meal. Then, if we can take advantage of your hospitality another night, we will return to our communities tomorrow morning."

So it was settled; they had some time to rest and get ready for the next meeting having no idea how much more they could all take.

Then Kurak'Kahn turned to Ogima Adoeete and Is'Taqa. "Thank you for your service. The next matter that we must discuss does not affect the Brothers. If you would like to return to your village, I am sure High Protector Acaraho will make the arrangements."

Acaraho stepped outside and asked First Guard Awan to escort the Brothers out and see that their ponies were brought around immediately.

"It grieves me not to see you off myself, but I will

come and visit you shortly. Safe passage," Acaraho told the Brothers.

Ogima Adoeete wondered if Kurak'Kahn would ever let it be known that Adia had saved them all. The High Council had not been able to come to a unanimous decision about Khon'Tor's punishment. They were stymied. The first law stated that the needs of the community came before the needs of the one. There was no doubt that Khon'Tor deserved punishment—perhaps even banishment as the Overseer had implied. But were the crimes of any one person ever important enough to destroy a community over? Was the punishment of any one person worth the resultant bloodshed and chaos that would no doubt ensue—perhaps lasting generations?

Anyone who was listening properly would have realized that Kurak'Kahn had merely opened the floor for Khon'Tor to make a case for why they should not banish him. The Overseer never stated that they had decided to do so.

They had been deadlocked. It was Kurak'Kahn alone who wanted to banish Khon'Tor. The others had stood firmly against it for all the reasons Adia had stated. They had been hoping that Khon'Tor would give up something in his defense that would allow them to agree on a lesser punishment. Chief

Ogima Adoeete patted Kurak'Kahn on the arm as he turned to leave.

"Kurak'Kahn. Your people are strong and powerful, and I am grateful for the peace between us. We share the same reverence for the Great Spirit and gratitude for all we have been given. But your people will have to change to survive, Overseer. Nothing in creation can stand still; change comes to us all whether we choose it or not. And it will be Leaders such as Acaraho and Adia who will guide your people through the challenges ahead."

On their way out, Is'Taqa turned to Adia, "So now what, Adia? What will you do now?"

"I will do as I have always done. I will live my life and find joy and happiness where I can. Because the truth is, we are all flawed. We all fail and we hurt others in the process, and there is no way to make everything fair. Sometimes, the only way to get through it is to get back up each time we are knocked down and continue doing the best we can. And when we are back on our own feet, we reach behind us to help another get back on theirs as well.

Both Chiefs knew she was referring to Khon'Tor. Somehow, she had found some faith in him still, despite his crimes against her.

As Khon'Tor filed past, Adia stopped him and said, "Go home to your new mate, Khon'Tor. Build a life of happiness for yourself and for her. And Acaraho and I will do the same."

As Khon'Tor stepped past him, Acaraho said solemnly, "Welcome back, Khon'Tor."

Khon'Tor took it in the spirit given. It was an acknowledgment by Acaraho that Khon'Tor had been given his life and his leadership back. So in reply, he simply said, "Thank you, Commander."

Everything had been set to zero. The circle of power that was the leadership of the People, that had been split apart by avarice, spite, and resentment, had just been healed and made whole by the Healer's words. It was a testament to all of them that love was the most powerful force in creation.

Acaraho reflected on the wisdom of Adia's words. Change came hard for the People. But he could see that their ways, though these allowed them to function and survive, would have to change if they were to avoid the extinction the High Council had talked about.

Adia had spoken of Acaraho being able to lead the People, and Acaraho felt the same about her. The Second Law, that the leadership could only be passed to a blood heir, was flawed. If the People did not find a way to change, adapt, grow, they would vanish from Etera.

CHAPTER 11

With not that much time until they met again, most everyone returned in groups to their quarters. Khon'Tor calculated that he had time for a quick visit to Tehya. He found her napping when he entered and did not wish to wake her. He stretched out beside her and lay there, still in shock about what had happened. His life had been taken from him and handed back in the space of a morning by the very person he had wronged the most.

He was still Khon'Tor, the Leader of the People of the High Rocks. He still had his freedom. He still had Tehya. Possibilities that he had relinquished now reappeared in front of him. He had time to grow and cherish his relationship with this surprising young female sleeping next to him. He had time to produce an heir to follow him. He had time to make amends to Adia and Acaraho—if that were possible.

And the others? Adia had absolved him of his crimes against her, but what of the others? He would have to find a way somehow to make amends; he could not allow himself to forget them and what they must surely be suffering.

Khon'Tor thanked the Great Spirit for his deliverance and vowed not to squander his second chance —his final chance—at redemption.

Tehya stirred and woke to find him next to her. She wrapped her arms around him and drew close. "Have you come back for good now, Adoeete?"

He knew she meant for the rest of the afternoon, but it struck him how appropriate her words were. "No, Tehya, I have only a few minutes, then I must return to meet with the High Council again. Would you not like to meet some of the other females to pass your time with while I am away? And I told you not to call me that," he added, smiling. He knew she was teasing him.

"No, I am fine here. But I hurt, Adoeete."

"I am so sorry. Do you wish me to ask the Healer to come and tend to you?"

"No, it will pass. But I do not think I can be with you for a few days now." She seemed to be apologizing.

"Oh no, of course not. Do not worry about that. We have a lifetime together, and we will have all the opportunities we want for lovemating." And Khon'Tor assured her that he was not going anywhere—at least now he could say that with assurance.

She curled up into a ball and drifted back to sleep. He covered her up, rose gingerly, and left to take a walk outside instead, not wishing to disturb her rest again.

Khon'Tor had been cooped up in Kthama for some time, but coming up the path was a young male whom he soon recognized as Nootau, followed closely by Nadiwani.

The Leader greeted them. "Hello. Have you been down to the Great River?"

"We were out looking for Kweeuu. He has been wandering off more and more, but this time he has been gone a long while." Nootau was referring to the giant grey wolf, once the tiny, fluffy cub that Oh'Dar had brought into the community. Kweeuu was their last connection to Oh'Dar, and it grieved them both that they saw him so seldom.

"He is no doubt off enjoying himself, Nootau. I would not worry about it. I am sure he will return at some point.

"Nadiwani, I wonder if you might help me. My new mate, Tehya," Khon'Tor did not know how to proceed delicately. "She is having some —discomfort."

Nadiwani nodded her understanding. "I will bring you some Willowbark tea, Khon'Tor. You will need to make a small fire to heat it, but it will help her with her pain. I will be glad to help her brew it, if that is alright with you?"

"If you do not mind. Thank you, Nadiwani," replied Khon'Tor, and he walked on.

The sky was a clear blue; the stars would be beautiful that night. Khon'Tor vowed to coax Tehya out here one way or another so they could enjoy them together. This was her home now, and he wanted her to see how beautiful their part of Etera was.

In all the years, it was the first time Khon'Tor had ever had a real conversation with Nadiwani, let alone asked for her help. No matter. Nadiwani was not going to miss any opportunity to mend relationships. Despite her practical and more abrupt approach, she had the same Healer's heart for helping others.

Nootau looked at Nadiwani, confused by Khon'-Tor's friendliness. After a lifetime of being ignored by the Leader, Khon'Tor was speaking with him now as if they had always conversed.

They continued past Khon'Tor and up the path back to Kthama.

Once again, the High Council members and community Leaders had reassembled in the meeting room.

The earlier matters now concluded, they came together to talk about the Wrak-Ayya, not as they had surmised it to be—the Waschini threat—but as the very real threat of extinction if they did not find a way to bring diversity to their pairing combinations. Adia had joined them, and Acaraho was present as High Protector.

"We are all tired, so let us get to the topic at hand. Everyone who is here was in the first meeting, except for Adia. We asked you to attend, Healer, as the danger we are facing will require all of our creativity to resolve," said Kurak'Kahn, acknowledging her role. "All Healers will be included in future matters of this magnitude.'

Kuruk'Kahn then explained the issue to Adia, adding, "If the lines of parentage begin to cross, we will start to see frailty, even deformities in our offspring. We have far less than seven generations in which to figure out a solution."

The others had already heard this, but Adia had not.

If what he is saying is true, it will be the end of the People. Adia shuddered in dread that Kurak'Kahn might next be going to suggest that the Wrak-Ayya usher in a return to the dark time between their people and the Brothers, the Wrak-Wavarra.

Reminding himself that he was still the Leader of his people, Khon'Tor spoke up. "We will do as you asked and search for forgotten communities of the People or the Sarnonn. But you are right that it will take some time. What are we to do in the meantime? Is there another solution?"

Kurak'Kahn now had to get to the point of this second meeting. He took a deep breath. "If we cannot find new groups of the People to pair with, we will have to consider less attractive alternatives or perish. There are—limited options."

Everyone in the room already understood—a return to the Wrak-Wavara, the Age of Darkness.

It was a time of shame for the People. Even though they were descendants of the Sarnonn, the huge hulking Sasquatch, clearly the People and the Sarnonn were not the same.

How the People came to be was not spoken of except in the smallest, most sacred of circles. The few who knew the story knew that Kurak'Kahn was proposing a descent back into darkness.

The stories handed down told that eons ago, at the time of the Ancients, the Brothers and the Sarnonn Sasquatch did not live in direct relationship; the tribes kept to themselves, avoiding each other and having virtually no interaction. They shared no language and kept to their respective territories. When a crisis befell the Sarnonn—when their survival was threatened, just as Kurak'Kahn was now warning would happen to the People—they had done what they had to do to ensure the continuation of their kind.

The Sarnonn discovered that the two tribes could interbreed. Word traveled to the others in the area.

Slowly, over time, the population was re-established, except that the offspring were hybrids—part Brother part Sarnonn. Smaller than the original Sasquatch but built more like the Brothers, they inherited the best attributes of each. They retained most of the strength of the Sarnonn but in a smaller, less bulky package. They seemed brighter than their pure Sasquatch ancestors. Though still resistant to change, they were somewhat more adaptive, more inclined to innovate, and their manual dexterity was greatly improved. As a result of all these differences, considerable cultural changes had also taken place over time.

They became known to themselves and the Brothers as *the People*.

The Sarnonn Sasquatch, like the People, were honorable, peace-loving creatures. They bore no natural aggression and lived in harmony. What they had been driven to do to ensure their survival was a source of great shame to them. For that shame, the truth of Wrak-Wavara was passed down only from Leader to Leader, and through the line of High Council Overseers.

And now, this elite group was listening to the High Council Overseer propose a return to barbarism?

"Kurak'Kahn," said Lesharo'Mok, shaking his head in disbelief. "Surely you do not mean to end the peace between the Brothers and us?"

"If we end up with it being the only solution

available, as it was for the Sarnonn, we will do everything we can to avoid violence. However, I am not sure the Brothers can help."

Yuma'qia spoke next, "Our blood has been mingled with the Brothers since the time of Wrak-Wavara. Even if we do find hidden pockets of our people, their numbers will be limited, and also depending on where they are located, an exchange among the People may not be feasible.

"We do not know how the Sarnonn are faring. We do not know how large their numbers are, or where they might be found. We do not know that they even exist; we have only rumors. It is possible that they could travel the same road our ancestors did. Or, we could enlist their help in diversifying our blood."

Everyone was imagining the outcome. If they mixed their blood back with the Sarnonn Sasquatch, they would gain strength and size, but would they not be stepping backward in dexterity and innovation? If enlisting the help of the Brothers might not be an option and breeding with the Sarnonn Sasquatch would only take them backward, then that left them only one direction to go if the People were not to die out.

The room fell silent. They looked around the room at one another. Everyone was thinking the same thing, but no one wanted to say the word.

Waschini.

The People considered the Waschini to be monsters, so the idea of crossing their lines with a people so aggressive and heartless would come up against a stone wall of resistance.

Adia thought of Oh'Dar. Both she and Nadiwani had noticed that even as an offspring, he was that much more inquisitive than his counterparts. He combined items in ways no one else thought of; he was more inventive, more creative, and he had finer manual dexterity.

Interbreeding with the Waschini would take them further in the same physical direction as had breeding with the Brothers. They would lose physical strength, probably the ability to navigate using Etera's magnetic currents, but gain in dexterity. Adia saw nothing in Oh'Dar of the terrible traits associated with the Waschini, but he was only one example against story after story that others told of their cruelty.

So much had happened in so few days. Everyone in the room had been taxed in every respect. And now they were presented with this seemingly insurmountable problem looming in their future and for which every solution carried a serious drawback.

They did not have time to set it aside to think

about later. The People had to act if they were going to survive.

Noting the slumped postures and tired faces, Acaraho spoke up. "Kurak'Kahn, the day is long gone. As Khon'Tor said, we will do our part in trying to locate others of our kind. If we find Sarnonn populations, how are we to proceed?"

"Since we must consider all options, and because the distances we may have to travel are likely to be far, in that situation, I would ask that whoever finds them tries to establish initial contact. It will take time because there is no quick and easy solution. Hopefully, we share enough of a root language to be able to communicate. The more we know, the better we will be prepared to decide which path we should choose," answered Kurak'Kahn.

"Let us see what we can discover by this season next year. We will send out messengers when we are ready to reconvene. May we meet here again, Acaraho? It is fairly central, even though still a long distance for those of the Great Pines and the High Red Rocks."

Kurak'Kahn had asked Acaraho rather than Khon'Tor, the one to whom he should properly have posed the question.

"Khon'Tor?" asked Acaraho, acknowledging that he was still their Leader.

"Yes, you are welcome here. It will be a smaller complement—nothing on the scale of the Ashwea Awhidi."

With that, Kurak'Kahn closed the meeting, and everyone headed out in their respective directions. In the morning, the High Council members would all go their separate ways.

Eventually, Khon'Tor, Adia, and Acaraho were the only ones still in the room. Adia remained seated, too tired to move.

"I do not think I can take any more," she said.

Khon'Tor spoke up, addressing Adia. "Let us all get some rest. Tomorrow we should address the People as a matter of closure. I am thinking of a light-hearted gathering. This Ashwea Awhidi has brought more than its share of surprises."

For the first time Adia could remember, Khon'Tor had spoken to her as an equal, not an adversary. He had made a movement toward peace, and she was not going to ignore it.

"Yes, that's a great idea. And you have a lovely new mate waiting for you," she said with a smile. Khon'Tor could sense in her words genuine happiness for him.

"And so do you, Healer," he added, acknowledging that Acaraho and Adia had also recently been paired.

"We have not even had time to—celebrate," commented Acaraho. And they chuckled.

Somehow all the years of animosity and pain had

slid into the background. The healing power of Love and Surrender had given the leadership of the People of the High Rocks the chance of a new beginning.

Khon'Tor returned to his quarters to find his new mate sitting more comfortably, sipping a bowl of Willow Bark tea.

"Where did you get that?" he asked, thinking that he probably knew the answer.

"Nadiwani, the Healer's Helper, brought it to me. She even showed me how to brew it. It has helped a lot, Adoeete, thank you," she said, a quirky little smile on her lips.

He could see she was going to continue calling him that just to tease him. He did not mind. He knew it was her way of being playful. It had none of the challenge in it that it would have had coming from Hakani.

"Do you think you are up to coming outside? The stars will be beautiful, and I want you to see them."

She nodded and set aside her tea.

Once outside, Khon'Tor took her up to the high point. Together they lay under the stars and marveled at the beauty of creation. Tehya rested her head against his chest, soothed by the rhythm of his heartbeat. Khon'Tor was filled with gratitude. He had so closely come to losing it all.

He tried to keep his other crimes out of his mind; how he now wished that he could undo what he had done to Tar'sa of the Deep Valley, and Kayah from the Far High Hills, who was now paired with Akule. And the one whose name he did not know, whom he had violated right here, outside Kthama. He had no idea how far the Great Spirit's forgiveness reached, but he prayed it would be far enough to cover all his sins.

And even if there was forgiveness from the Great Spirit, could he find forgiveness for himself? Adia's silence had protected him all these years and revoking her accusation had set him free from the consequences of what he had done to her. But surely a debt for his other travesties would someday come due. Khon'Tor put the thought out of his mind, trying to return to the brief time of peace with his precious Tehya.

While Khon'Tor and Tehya were resting underneath the stars, Adia and Acaraho had returned to her quarters. They were both exhausted, and though they longed to consummate their pairing in waking time, they were not up to it. Instead, they too lay together, giving thanks for the unprecedented change that had just taken place in the lives of them all.

CHAPTER 12

Everyone sat in great anticipation of what Khon'Tor would say. The Ashwea Awhidi had ended. Excited conversation filled the air. The new members of the community sat with their new mates and new families. Though the hard, physical work of cleaning up and re-sorting was wrapping up, the real work lay in helping those new to Kthama adjust to the different surroundings and way of life at the High Rocks.

Nimida sat with Mapiya and the other females of Adia's inner circle, Haiwee, Pakuna, and Nadiwani. Nootau sat between Acaraho and Adia. When they were not looking, Adia could not help study Nimida and Nootau. They had looked identical at birth, but now no one would know they were related. Nimida had taken after Adia, and Nootau after Khon'Tor. She knew she would have to make sure that no interest developed between them—but how? The High Council had paired them with the idea that they would do well together. She would have to tell them the truth, that they were brother and sister, and sooner, not later.

Khon'Tor entered with his new mate in tow. Everyone watched as they came in. There was no denying that Khon'Tor was a magnificent male, and the female walking next to him was a stark contrast to him with her smaller stature and delicate build. She favored the Brothers' side of the People's background, to be sure.

In a way, it was almost frightening how things had changed between Khon'Tor, Adia, and Acaraho. Not as quick to forgive as Adia, to a point Acaraho still had his guard up around Khon'Tor. But he knew they had been given a chance to reunite the leadership of the People, and he would not let his reservations poison the opportunity. Seeing the obvious sweetness between Khon'Tor and his mate gave him great pause. Based on his earlier suspicions about what went on between Khon'Tor and Hakani, this was not the relationship he had expected to see developing.

Khon'Tor stopped by and asked if Tehya could join them for the moment while he opened the meeting. Adia scooted over to make room next to her for the young female.

Khon'Tor stepped to the front, bearing his

Leader's staff in one hand and raising his other as was his custom. The conversation slowed to a stop, and the air was charged with excitement and well-being.

They could not put their finger on it, but Khon'Tor was different. He was still a commanding figure, but something was missing; the angry edge was gone. This was a softer version of him. Not knowing what had transpired between the three Leaders, everyone attributed it to his finally taking a new mate. And they would not be entirely wrong, for truly Tehya had touched a place in Khon'Tor that would turn out to bring him his greatest blessings, as well as his next greatest challenges.

"Good morning. It has been quite a celebration, hasn't it?" Khon'Tor asked the crowd, and they did not disappoint him; a rousing agreement met him in response.

"We have lost some of our members; it is true. And they are off on their new adventure, going through the first days of getting used to their new lives just as those who have joined us are doing here.

"I know that you will all welcome our new members and help them feel at home. Kthama is their home now, and we are their people, and we are grateful for them all." He could not help but look at Tehya when he said this.

"We are all tired, but we have many blessings to celebrate. We are expecting a plentiful harvest, which will replenish our exhausted stores. And before long, we will have new offspring keeping their parents up at night and toddling through our corridors."

They had never heard him joke like this. This was not the Leader they had known all along. The armor of anger was gone, and he no longer bristled as he always had, even when at rest.

Tehya could feel people staring at her, but she had no idea why. She did not know how grateful they were for whatever this small wraith of a female had done to soothe the steely, prickly Alpha.

"We have much to celebrate, not the least of which is the pairing of High Protector Acaraho and our Healer Adia. And I have my own reasons for being grateful." Khon'Tor reached his hand out, inviting Acaraho, Adia, and Tehya to stand with him.

Adia took Tehya's hand and led her along, not sure she would understand the cue. She placed the young female to Khon'Tor's left, and he took her hand and pulled her closer to him.

The new leadership of the High Rocks stood before the People. Khon'Tor, his mate Tehya, High Protector Acaraho, and their Healer, Adia. Ostensibly, nothing other than the addition of Tehya had changed, but everything was different.

They saw a softness in Khon'Tor that they had never known possible. They saw a mate for their Leader, who was nothing like Hakani. Who seemed content to stand next to him, not because he was the Leader of the largest community of the People, and not because being his mate gave her a position of power in return. Whereas Hakani had been ambitious, Tehya seemed happy to be who she was. Finally, Khon'Tor would have a mate who did not challenge and thwart him at every turn. Perhaps now there could be peace in the Leader's Quarters and in the Leader's heart.

And then there were Acaraho and Adia. The couple that never should have been, a love that took root and grew against all the rules. The respect they had for High Protector Acaraho and the love they had for Adia had weathered all the controversy, speculation, and turmoil.

Adia knew her people would always believe that Acaraho was the father of Nootau. They would always think that she had failed at maintaining the purity required of her position as Healer. But she could live with it. Her community, for the moment, was safe. More than safe, it was on the brink of thriving. New blood, new beginnings, and new hope for the future. They did not know about the threat of their potential extinction, nor did they need to. That was a burden for their leadership to bear. There were several generations between then and now; they had time to find a solution, and she vowed that they would indeed find one.

Khon'Tor looked down the line and raised

Tehya's hand in his. Adia took Tehya's other hand in her own, and Acaraho's on her other side. Together they all raised their hands in unison, and the People cheered. Whatever was coming, they would face it together.

CHAPTER 13

Oh'Dar pulled Dreamer up outside the stables, the horse's hooves throwing up a cloud of dust as they came to a stop. The young man was enjoying one of his last rides on the huge beast before leaving.

Mr. Jenkins watched Oh'Dar with admiration. They had never talked about his past, but somewhere, the lad had learned how to ride with the best.

Oh'Dar smiled profusely as he led Dreamer inside for a rubdown and grooming. The young man's black leather hat and riding boots complemented his black hair, which, much to the chagrin of his grandmother, he had gone back to wearing longer.

Mrs. Morgan leaned against the fence next to Mr. Jenkins, also watching her grandson bring in the huge stallion. "Oh Jenkins, he's going to be a heartbreaker, that's for sure." She sighed heavily.

"Let's hope he keeps his head on straight and doesn't lose his heart while he's away," offered the stable master.

"I only want the best for him. Maybe his crush on Miss Blain was a good thing. Maybe it'll keep his mind off the local girls."

"It might keep his mind off the local girls, Miss Vivian, but I don't think much is going to keep the local girls' minds off him."

Mrs. Morgan frowned at Mr. Jenkins; his comments were not helping. "It's going to be quiet when he's gone. First Louis, now Grayson. Our home is going to be empty."

Mr. Jenkins put his arm around Mrs. Morgan and hugged her. "Well, maybe with everyone gone, you can stop calling me Jenkins and start calling me Ben," and he let his hand slip to her waist.

Mrs. Morgan blushed but made no motion to dislodge it. Instead, she looked up coyly and replied, "I think I could do that, yes, Ben."

Oh'Dar was working on Dreamer and watching Mr. Jenkins and his grandmother out of the corner of his eye. He liked what he was seeing. Perhaps his absence would turn out to be a good thing for the two of them.

The hired driver would be coming in two days to pick him up and cart him off to school. He had packed everything he could think of, including several changes of clothes and some money. It had taken him a while to understand that the coins had a common value and that they worked as a universal barter system. He was used to trading objects, each of which held its own value.

Fully recovered months ago from his earlier bout with illness, Oh'Dar was as ready for his new adventure as he was going to be. He had been through so many challenges, and he counted this as one more. But his family back home was weighing heavily on his mind, lately even more so than normal. He doubted he'd ever get over being homesick.

Oh'Dar was slightly older than his brother Nootau. He wondered if Nootau had taken a mate at the Ashwea Awhidi, which by now would have taken place. From reflecting on what he knew of the People directly and what Acaraho had taught him about their history, he calculated that the Waschini had shorter lifespans than the People. A large pairing celebration had not taken place all the time he was growing up, the only ones he remembered were quite a few years ago and had been very small by comparison to what he had heard they were usually like. The one that had just passed would have been quite a celebration.

The days passed quickly, and in no time, Oh'Dar was saying his goodbyes to his Waschini family. His grandmother squeezed him so hard he thought he would pop. Not one to show emotion, tears nevertheless ran down her beautiful, soft complexion.

Even Mr. Jenkins hugged him long and hard. "Grayson, remember what we talked about, to do with the young women. You have plenty of time to choose a wife. Concentrate on your studies and don't lose sight of your goals."

Mrs. Morgan was grateful to Mr. Jenkins for taking her grandson under his wing. Somehow it had more impact coming from a man. Whenever she tried to talk to him about girls, she felt that she came off as an old biddy.

Oh'Dar said his goodbyes to the rest of the Shadow Ridge family. Mrs. Thomas, the kitchen staff, all the farmhands, everyone had come out to wish him well. He handed Mr. Jenkins a wrapped package of sugar, telling him it was for Dreamer. Mrs. Thomas placed her hands on her hips in mock anger, well aware that he had been sneaking it out of the kitchen for some time.

As the carriage finally pulled away, Oh'Dar resigned himself to a very long trip. He would have a great deal of time to think, and he was not sure he liked that at all.

Fall turned to winter and winter to early Spring. Oh'Dar had not only adjusted to his new environment, but he was also thriving. He had quickly decided to dig in and accept the challenges that his life kept throwing him. His new resolve showed through in his outer appearance, too. He was more confident, so he walked taller and met others with his head held high. He still did not know who he was —Oh'Dar son of Adia the Healer of the People of the High Rocks, or Grayson Stone Morgan III, heir to the Morgan fortune—but he knew that whoever he was, it was up to him to create his own life.

His grandmother was a faithful correspondent, and each week brought at least one letter, if not two. He read and cherished every one he received from Shadow Ridge and saved them for re-reading. He could feel his grandmother's love through her writing. Oh'Dar knew that his absence was hard on her, and he was pleased at every reference to Mr. Jenkins. He hoped that the romance would continue to grow.

In the back of his mind, he knew that one day he would return to the People, for how long he did not know, because he missed his family and had to see Adia and Acaraho again and explain in person. But he grieved at the idea of leaving his grandmother alone again.

Miss Blain and Mr. Carter had done a fine job of preparing him. The Waschini field of medicine was different from how the People and the Brothers approached it, but he was becoming anxious to get back and start his apprenticeship with Dr. Miller.

Oh'Dar had only once been back to Shadow Ridge since he had come to the school the previous fall, but a summer break was due soon. In a new letter, his grandmother wrote that Dreamer had sired several new foals. Though they all had the promise of their magnificent sire, one colt in particular seemed a perfect copy of Dreamer. Oh'Dar could not wait to see the foal; they were calling him Lightning, and apparently, he would bring a high price.

Oh'Dar was enjoying hearing about life back home until the last paragraph.

"A large grey wolf has started showing up at Shadow Ridge."

PLEASE READ

I am humbled by your continued interest in my writing. If you enjoyed this book, I would very much appreciate your leaving a review. Reviews give potential readers an idea of what to expect, and they also provide useful feedback for authors. The feedback you give me, whether positive or not so positive, helps me to work even harder to provide the content you want to read.

If you would like to be notified when the other books in this series are available, or if you would like to join the mailing list, please subscribe to my monthly newsletter on my website at
https://leighrobertsauthor.com/contact.

Wrak-Ayya: The Age of Shadows is the first of three series in The Etera Chronicles.

The next book in this series is: Book Five: *Contact*

ACKNOWLEDGMENTS

Writing a book is a huge undertaking. Writing a series of books is on another scale altogether. Thank you to everyone who stood by me through this. There are many more books to come in this series so there is a lot more gratitude to come also!

I am especially grateful my editor has not abandoned me yet. She is a woman of great patience, as well as of great talent.